ALL FOR MOTHER

K. MOORE

Copyright © 2020 by K. Moore
All rights reserved.

Visit my website www.authorkmoore.com
Cover Designer: Ryan Schwarz, The Cover Designer, www.thecoverdesigner.com
Editor and Interior Designer: Jovana Shirley, Unforeseen Editing, www.unforeseenediting.com

No part of this book may be reproduced or transmitted in any form or by any means, electronic or mechanical, including photocopying, recording, or by any information storage and retrieval system without the written permission of the author, except for the use of brief quotations in a book review.

This book is a work of fiction. Names, characters, places, and incidents either are products of the author's imagination or are used fictitiously. Any resemblance to actual persons, living or dead, events, or locales is entirely coincidental.

ASIN: B08235WZW8
ISBN-13: 978-1-7328844-6-5
Paperback: 978-1-7328844-5-8, 978-1-7328844-4-1

For the father figures in my life, may you rest in peace:
NJT
JDM
JGB

"My father didn't tell me how to live;
he lived and let me watch him do it."

—Clarence Budington Kelland

ONE

I watch the procession of cars that line the asphalt road curving through the well-manicured lawns. The slight sway of the aged oaks shimmer dappled light across the tombstones, giving them an unearthly glow, as though their occupants had come out to welcome the new neighbor.

It starts with a funeral.

It always starts with a funeral.

Generally, they're meant to be sad affairs, lamenting the loss of a loved one or someone who, in some way, gained influence over others. They represent the ultimate proof of our mortality. Life can't move forward without death. After all, death—or at least, a good death—remains life's ultimate end goal. It amuses me that most go through life in fear of it and that this one thing influences decisions and clouds judgment.

But death surrounds us daily in one way or another. It's the only constant we have and share. A million souls parading through life, trying to be independent or unique, only to end up in the same place as everyone else—locked in a box six feet under or secured in a sealed jar. Either way, existence is snuffed and turned into dust as time continues without a care.

To measure the quality or success of time spent walking the earth, can it be by the amount of earthly possessions acquired, the number of people who mourn for you, or the length of the obituary placed in the newspaper?

I ponder this, not for the first time. Even the winged creatures hidden in the depths of the branches seem to hold their tongues, watching silently from lofty perches. Every now and again, one will break protocol and sing a short, sorrowful message across the way, adding an ethereal feeling to an already-somber mood.

The heat and humidity are stifling, and like many times before, I wish the AC worked. My beat-up off-red Jeep, a conspicuous addition to the neat row of newer and sleeker cars, has definitely seen better days. It, however, has been a steadfast companion, having cemented my lifelong loyalty during my college days by always being there, unlike the *family* I surround myself with now. Looking at the sun-worn paint, I'm reminded of my father and how he gifted the beast to me all those years ago. I'd probably have traded up before now if I could hold down a job long enough to afford it. Or maybe I'd keep it out of pure nostalgia. Either way, more debt isn't an option.

The grumble of engines turning over and small puffs of exhaust break the spell of my past. A black hearse passes slowly on its way to the head of the line, signaling the start to this formal end of my father's life and, by extension, the end of his influence on me. I follow along, going through the motions of parking while swept up with the nameless faces trailing the flag-draped casket with its honor guard to the gravesite. Camouflaged in black attire, I cling to the shadows, not wanting to draw attention from family and other close friends whose sympathy would be unwelcome.

Family and close relatives' friends sit at the front. Their sorrow is on full display as it hangs like a cold, dense fog crossing the marshes, concealing both predator and prey. Taking advantage of the shield of grief, I become invisible against the back wall, lost in the congregation of bodies. No one will notice.

I hope no one notices.

Standing off to one side at the rear of the crowd, I watch, mesmerized, as a baby bird braves the ring of predators to land on the wreath centered in front of the coffin. The military padre continues his sermon, defining life and death and life after death, not aware of the latest addition to his flock. The bird hops from one foot to the other, pecking at the flower arrangement until the uniformed soldiers lift the flag from the coffin, causing the tiny creature to freeze in fear. It raises its head hesitantly, cocking it slightly to the side to watch the men. I'm enamored with its courage. As if reading my thoughts, it shifts its penetrating gaze to me.

I stare into those dark orbs, bedazzled. It's as though it were speaking to me, like it knows me. For whatever bizarre reason, I feel a kinship with it. The bird opens its beak for a single sorrowful call, trying to tell me something but I don't know what. After what seems like a lifetime, it spreads its miniature black wings wide and disappears with a flutter. The motion jars me from my thoughts and highlights my solitude.

Pathetic.

A sharp crack resounding through the air, coupled with the wafting scent of gunpowder, brings me back to the now. My body involuntarily flinches with each subsequent echo of guns, saluting the life and service of my father. Birds, formerly happy with their unobtrusive overwatch, take to the sky, squawking their protest from above. The crescendo plays out until we're left with only a moment's silence before a bugle plays the first notes of "Butterfield's Lullaby."

Time stands eerily still. It's in this intense silence that I feel my mind bolster my resolve to sort my crappy life. I'm not sure how I'll do this, but I know I must.

A shiver travels up my spine as I feel the spirits of the cemetery's slumbering ghosts waken to welcome their comrade-in-arms. Corner to corner, the flag is folded with military precision until it's nothing more than a life reflected in geometry, a triangular prism. Gloved hands gently hold the material as they offer the token to my widowed mother.

Tears line the faces of those around me. I can't help but cringe at the irony. My father served his country proud. If only he'd served and protected those closest to him with the same fervor.

TWO

"Ash, good of you to make it."

The voice startles me from behind. I was hoping to sneak in to witness the burial and then escape, unnoticed. High expectations to be sure and rather idiotic, given the openness of the cemetery and my less than austere demeanor. I turn slowly and mask my expression with well-practiced neutrality.

"Uncle John." There's an uncomfortable pause as we watch each other before I sigh, and manners ingrained from my Southern upbringing kick in by rote. "How are you?"

His lips turn up into a forced smile, displaying yellowed teeth. "It's been a while, young'un. You're looking …"

His unfinished statement hangs on the humid air, causing me to flinch, break eye contact, and look beyond him. I don't want to read the disappointment and perhaps the loathing in his eyes. Sometimes, no words speak the loudest, and it's obvious he definitely wants to be heard.

Those standing around my mother—offering what I expect to be the requisite messages of sympathy and condolences, as dictated by Southern niceties—are dispersing.

The blonde hair of my sister catches the light. Her face is framed by large, dark sunglasses, and from this distance,

I can't make out if they're hiding red rims or crinkled mirth. Judging by the pursed lips and frown as she gazes in my direction before moving her attention back to Mother, it's probably resigned annoyance.

Trapped, I stand stiffly with my uncle, who is acting as a warden by my side, nodding at the expressionless faces as the dwindling crowd moves toward their cars.

They probably don't recognize me.

Or maybe they do.

Either way, I don't care.

Or so I tell myself.

When I cast a look over my shoulder, the whispered words and arm-nudging tell me they do.

I blink back the nonexistent tears, inwardly cringing at the adolescent response. I didn't cry at the news of my father passing or as I just watched his body being lowered into the ground. But a few stares and non-stares and hushed conversation have me reliving those terrible times of my late youth, those I promised myself I'd forget. That's what shakes me.

The arm of my mother trembles as she takes my cheek in her hand, offering a teary smile. Wrinkles mar her once-beautiful face. I blink twice and glance behind her to Bel, my sister, as she watches the exchange with a slight scowl. She was the one who reached out to me, trying to convince me to come back and bury the hatchet when our father was on his deathbed.

But stubbornness is something that runs in the family.

I can't forgive her for her words over the years. And for standing against me when I needed my sister, my friend, at my side. And I don't forgive her for aligning herself with our father and their narrow-minded views of the world, its politics and the impact it had on me and my life. Time passing can be cruel, but the souring of our relationship seems but a tainted minute that will probably span our lifetime. I wish it had been different or could be different, but judging by the tenseness in her neck, more than likely brought about by a hard jaw ... well, there you go.

As if she can hear my thoughts, Bel's eyebrows knit together, fine lines on her forehead evident. I cast my gaze back down to Mother. Her face is masked with layered makeup, caked on, displaying an embalmer's flair.

The aging process has not been kind.

Her eyes are weary, probably a result of the countless tears she must've shed for my father leading up to his passing. But it's more than that. Her body is ... frail. Either the trauma of being so close to death has caused this or time has accelerated exponentially as her years have advanced. The well-tailored clothes don't conceal her weight loss and fragility.

I gently take the gnarled fingers of her bony hand in mine and lower them from my face.

"Mother, it's nice to see you." My voice cracks on the last two words, threatening to send my emotions over the edge. I don't know what's going on with me or why I'm reacting this way. Feelings I've kept suppressed over the years continue to come unbidden and threaten to bubble to the fore. "I really wish it were under different circumstances."

Bel harrumphs and turns away slightly, appearing to want to be anywhere but here. I don't blame her.

The sad smile on my mother's face says everything and nothing. She appears conflicted as she takes a step closer, the sadness from moments before tightening, pulling the creases around her eyes. "I'm so glad you could make it, Ash. It's been too long."

I nod, unable to speak, swallowing the hard lump in my throat as her skeletal arms embrace me in a cloddish hug, reminiscent of strangers.

"It has," I whisper into her hair and take a deep breath, inhaling the tinny, chemical scent of hair spray and the starch of her jacket. It's a different smell from my youth, but under it all, my olfactory senses pick up a hint of camphor, mixed in faintly with the floral undertones of her signature perfume.

She steps back on unsteady feet, releasing me from her hold. Bel hurriedly places a hand under the crook of her elbow to support her.

"You're joining us for lunch? We've reserved the dining hall at the lodge." Her words are said quietly with the hesitance of a mother coaxing a scared young child. "It's what your father would have wanted."

My body stiffens at her words. The lodge. I'm sure it was what he wanted. How suitably pretentious of him.

Bel's demeanor shifts slightly, appearing more rigid, if that's even possible. Her nose screws up, and with a slight tilt of her head, she sends an unspoken message, saying my attendance at the wake would be a bad idea. I don't need her silent cues. I can easily make this decision myself. The scrutiny of family friends and distant relatives during this foray hasn't been comfortable—and we're in an open cemetery; I can't imagine what it would be like, trapped within the confines of four walls.

"No, Mom. I don't think I can."

The trees sway slightly as a breeze passes through, their rustling leaves the only sound filling the uncomfortable moment that follows my refusal. I watch as the shadows from the movement play games on the ground beyond my mother, sister, and uncle, wondering what I can do or say to escape this awkwardness.

I clear my throat, about to ramble something about having to leave. To do something. To be anywhere but here ... or God forbid, the wake. The reality of it all is too somber; I have nowhere to go, nothing to look forward to.

No job.
No family.
Nothing.

"Where are you staying, Ash?" Mother's words break me from the spiraling dark thoughts.

ALL FOR MOTHER

My eyes find hers again, and I'm surprised to glimpse the reflection of regret in them. But are they hers ... or mine? Over the years, I've felt lost and alone, without purpose. The breaking of familial bonds decades prior left me bereft, but it took me a good while to notice and then to finally work out what it was. As I look into eyes so similar to mine, thoughts and possibilities whirl crazily, almost haphazardly, until a spark of something erupts, resulting in an indescribable yearning.

She might need me and ...

I think I need her. I wish it were that easy.

"You should come home." Her words come slowly and softly. "Stay with me for a while."

It's like she read my mind. But is this what I want? So much time has passed, and I don't know if either Mother or I have changed so dramatically over the years. I'd like to mend the rift, and it would be easier without Father.

The words are barely out of Mother's mouth before the protests from my uncle and sister start overriding my answer.

"No! Mom, no."

"Lizzy?"

"I-I booked a hotel down off the highway. I wasn't sure what was appropriate ..."

"No. Nonsense. I think this will be good. It's time." Mother pats Bel's arm and gives it a quick squeeze. "It's time we let go of the past."

My shoulders straighten as I pull myself to my full height and take a deep breath. Maybe this could work. Me staying might be the answer I've been searching for to take that first step to reconciling the past. I could stay with her and regroup for a few weeks, maybe a month. Apply for a new job, get my life in order, and be ready for the next stage—whatever that entails. And in the process, I can be a friendly ear or a body in the now-empty house. I'll be there to help her avoid the overwhelming isolation and loneliness. We can be bound together in that in-between period of not knowing what comes next. Without my father's overbearing presence, it might even be a chance to rekindle the relationship lost after my youth.

I know with conviction what I need to do. To take a chance and let go of the past. To move forward.

My lips turn up into a smile as I remember the bird on Father's coffin. I think I now know what message it was trying to relay. It was asking me to forgive.

"Are you sure?" I ask hesitantly, trying not to show my growing enthusiasm.

Bel's sigh is resolute. She places a caring arm around Mother to usher her toward the car. "Come, Mother. We need to get going if we're going to make it to the lodge in time."

My mother nods, donning the mask of a grieving widow once again. "The key is where it has always been. Let yourself in if I'm not home."

They turn together, and I watch in silence as they slowly walk away.

"Ash." My uncle brings my attention back to him. He stands with his hands in the trouser pockets of an old brown suit, watching his sister and mine depart.

If it wasn't for the severity of the moment, the warning tone of his voice, combined with the previous grumblings, would almost make me laugh. It's not as though Mother is asking a stranger into her home. I am her flesh and blood. The vital fluid that flows through my veins is the same as hers. Our physical makeup is shared. A bloodline, also shared.

"Don't screw this up."

It's good to see that after all this time, some things are the same. But there's only one way to change people's perceptions of me—not that I really care.

That's a lie.

I must care, or why would I be considering this? Two decades of my life was spent as part of this family, that time almost equal to the part that I was not. Can I do this?

ALL FOR MOTHER

The thoughts of solitude I had moments before my father was lowered in the ground come back tenfold.

Mother.

I can help Mother.

"No, Uncle, I won't."

THREE

I'm here, in the house that's replaced the one of my youth, staying with my mother. It's modest and clinical and very, very beige. Not to my taste at all. It does, however, suit my mother down to a T, but I've always wondered why my father put up with it. His personality is only on display in the study while the rest of the house looks like it's been frozen in time from some '50s or '60s Suzy Homemaker magazine.

The house is the largest of the smaller domiciles on the country club estate, something pointed out with swagger to anyone who might have cause to judge. It boasts all the rooms and amenities, which made it easier during those infrequent times I did visit and bring friends. Warmth and all of those little things that make a house a home are what's missing. No notches on a doorframe to show the growth of us children. No artwork, cards, or recent photos pinned on the fridge. No magazines or papers lying around, showcasing casual living. Everything has its place, hidden away, unseen. It's just plain sterile.

My biggest criticism is, there's no color. That, and it's dark. She keeps the expensive white plantation shutters closed at all times. They mark the areas where sunshine or fresh air should flow through, standing out in stark contrast to the … beige. Even during the happier times, before I was made *persona non grata*, we'd congregate in the formal dining room to share a holiday meal, and the house would remain in partial shadow. It was a standing joke of mine that we were really a family of vampires and that our day-walker abilities left us when we aged. I'd laugh this off to visitors, and she and my father would always purse their lips, shake their heads, and mutter apologies for my blasphemous sense of humor. She'd never open the blinds though to prove me wrong.

I silently berate myself for drudging up memories that could result in me spiraling down the rabbit hole of negativity, and I remind myself that she wants me here, that I want to be here. Should it matter how she wants to live, and am I really in a position to pass judgment? It's not as though I have a home to decorate and call my own. But coming back and seeing that not much has changed within the house and the way she's been living over the years has me wondering if there's a chance she can really forgive and accept the past.

The bedroom I've been allocated is in the back, which totally makes sense. I'll be out of the way in the event anyone comes over, meaning we'll both get our privacy. The room would be decent-sized if not for the overly large pieces of furniture occupying the space. When they downsized, they only sacrificed square footage—and paint color—and found different ways to store their belongings.

I step through the doorway and inhale. Mothballs and old age permeate the whole house, but the scent seems somewhat stronger back here. Some might say the musty odor mothballs emit *is* the same as old age, but it's not. There's a distinct difference. The smell is a combined fragrance of soured milk, cloying flatulence, and … death.

For the first time, I question my sanity for taking this on. Thirty-five and moving back home—even if it's for a few weeks—I might as well hang a sign around my neck saying, *Loser*, or, *Life Failure*. No fame or fortune. Not married. No family of my own. Not even a significant other. Not even a pet. None of the things most my age have and hold dear. Just life experiences masking scars and deep regrets. But here I am, with Mother's years of hoarding, evidenced by the overfilled drawers and limited hanging space to greet me.

Sweaters in their shipping plastic, price tags still attached, sit side by side, some yellowing with what could be their almost half-century age. I begin to push a few out of the way to make space for my belongings, only to hesitate and open my suitcase on the timber luggage rack instead. In all honesty, my limited things won't take up much space, but the remembered anxiety and grumbles from the last time I moved anything within these walls echoing through the room suggest the rack is the best choice. For now. It's probably wise for me to wait before touching anything.

The mattress doesn't give when I sit, hunched, bringing elbows to my knees and clasping my head in my hands. My father's funeral was uncomfortable and unwelcoming to the nth degree, but there was a moment where I felt the darkness in my soul lighten. Maybe it was from releasing the burden of carrying around all of his expectations. With him gone, there's this inkling of hope and the formulation of ideas showcasing an alternate path to my destructive life to date. One that I'll see through and one that hopefully will help bring me closure to my tumultuous youth.

Soft shuffling with the telltale drag sounds from down the hall and announces her approach, but I don't look up until she speaks.

"Ash, you getting settled?" she asks, leaning on the wall for support.

I nod, take a deep breath, and stand. The forced smile pulls tightly around my eyes. "Yeah. I didn't bring much, just a few bags of clothes. So, it won't take long. Thanks again for letting me stay, Mom."

"Nonsense. I'm looking forward to the company. You can clear space in those two top drawers over there if you'd like," she says, indicating the cherry wood dresser.

It probably doesn't cross her mind to realize the suitcase and medium brown bag on the floor obviously contain more than can fit in the drawers. At least it's something.

"Sure, Mom. Thanks."

Her eyes light up, and she slowly turns to leave. "Supper'll be ready in fifteen minutes. It's not much, just some leftovers from lunch today. You've time to tidy yourself up. I'll see you at the table shortly."

My eyes follow her as she slowly walks away, hands reaching out to the wall every now and again to steady herself. Her knees knock together, and there's a sharp intake of breath that doubles as a whimper while she teeters on her legs. After a moment's pause and a resigned sigh, she continues on.

She really should be using some sort of walking aid. I thought this earlier, in the cemetery, but at the time, she had my sister to lean on. I'm sure if I'd raised that concern, I'd have been told in no uncertain terms to not be so ridiculous. It's a Southern thing, and I've seen it before, growing up around the church. Elderly ladies fighting the aging process, hoping a united front will keep it at bay. Using anything as a crutch in the battle would more or less be waving a white flag. Defeat. I wonder what their take is on broken bones received from a nasty fall. That might be an acceptable casualty in the war and an appropriate reason to be seen with a cane or wheeled walker.

She turns the corner to enter the kitchen, and I run my hands through my hair and groan with frustration.

Supper.

I forgot how she gets when family stays, and I should've expected something like this. Her little idiosyncrasies of everything having to be done a certain way, like eating at the exact same time every day and expecting everyone to adhere to a dress standard. As a kid, I wished she'd put the same amount of fussing into the food she served us. She hates to cook—and for good reason because her food is unimaginative and barely edible. Processed and high in salt and preservatives—a result of being a card-carrying member of the Campbell Soup generation, where household ingredients were measured in silver tins. A pantry missing the telltale red-and-white labels boasting blandness is, to her, not a real pantry at all.

At least there's something positive that came out of my father's wake. I just hope the food leftovers are edible.

The table's set when I enter the kitchen, and I silently scoff to see paper towels instead of place mats and coasters. Ornate silver flatware and glasses filled with water and ice complete the setting. There's no food, although the mouthwatering aroma wafting in suggests something has been prepared. Or heated, as evidenced by the long, dulcet tone coming from the microwave.

She's sitting, and she looks up expectantly with a practiced smile at my approach. The flicker in her eyes makes me feel a little bad for the second thoughts that were running through my mind about being here. She appears more like the mother of my youth, and for a second, I think I see some of the warmth directed toward me that's been missing for quite some time. It's gone in a blink, replaced by sorrow.

"Ash, the food's ready." Her hands are clasped in her lap as she waits patiently for me to take action.

I nod at her veiled instruction and grab the oven mitts on the countertop beside the oven. Going through the motions, I serve slices of meatloaf and vegetables onto plates before putting hers in front of her and sitting. With cutlery in my hand, my mouth waters as I wonder how long it's been since I've had something more than takeout. The knife slices through the tender meat, separating a bite-sized portion, and gently nudges it onto the fork's prongs when Mother clears her throat. My eyes meet hers, and I see the disappointment.

She reaches out and lays her hands open on top of the table, waiting for me to place mine in hers. "We should say a blessing."

"Yes, Mother." I school my expression to hide the grimace and place the cutlery down before gently clasping her hand.

I accept there's a higher power—God, if we need to name it. I'd like to think my connection to him is strong. That bird could've been a sign from God. I also believe in miracles and the power of positive thought. My youth was spent providing service to the church, but their actions toward me when I needed them most tempered my opinion on many traditions. I no longer subscribe to the extreme burden of church life and the belief to be seen genuflecting almost every second of the day.

"Heavenly Father …"

I close my eyes and only half-listen to her prayer of thanks. She's thankful Father's burial today went well. For friends and family who've seen her through the difficult times. And for me being here, returning to the fold.

"Amen."

My mind wanders as we eat. The reheating of the meatloaf has sucked out most of its moisture, but the dryness doesn't lessen its tastiness. By habit, I squirt almost half a bottle of ketchup on top. Mother watches in amusement, careful to cut small pieces of food. Very few of them make it to her mouth, the remainder pushed around on the plate.

Between bites, I watch her. She appears more relaxed than I've seen her in the past and definitely more so than in the cemetery. I can't imagine the hole that's been left with the absence of a husband who, since his retirement a decade prior, spent almost every day with her. It must have been lonely, leading up to his death. I wasn't in the picture, and Bel's decision to take a job and move her life to another part of the state years prior most likely made visits irregular.

For a woman whose life identity has been as wife and mother, what is she now? A widow? A grandmother? Both of these things are true, but are they something you wake up to every morning, knowing your daily purpose within those definitions?

"How long do you think you'll stay?" She wipes a stray hair off her face and twists a knuckle from the corner of an eye outward. Her sockets are sunken and rimmed by dark circles.

"I'm not sure. A week? Two? I'm between jobs, and I need to look for work and a new place to live." I shrug. "Who knows how long that will take? But I promise I won't be a nuisance. I'm here for you—to help or just hang out."

"That sounds nice."

I stand, retrieving the dishes, ready to scrape them off and stack them in the dishwasher.

"There's no need for you to do that. I can do it," she says, fussing with the napkin in front of her.

"No, Mother. It's fine. I'm sure I can handle cleaning a few dishes."

A tired smile graces her lips. "Okay then. If you say so."

The chair scrapes audibly over the tiles as she pushes it back and teeters in place after standing. I pause my ministrations to watch as she picks up her half-empty glass of water and slowly takes the ten steps to the cabinet on the opposite side of the kitchen. Shelves loaded with pharmaceutical and vitamin bottles are exposed once the door is opened, and I watch in fascination as she starts unscrewing lid after lid, swallowing pill after pill.

FOUR

"This is nice, Ash, having you here. I'm so glad you decided to stay," my mother says, spooning the warm liquid into her mouth.

It's been … tolerable.

Sort of. The past three days, we've been skirting around the heavy issues and tentatively trying to reacquaint ourselves with each other. It's been more awkward than anything else, but each day has been easier. It helps that when I've been in the house, I've been busy, going through the multitude of tasks she's written out for me.

I've managed to keep out of her way for the most part. Or I've tried. The house is in a state of disrepair under all the subterfuge and needs attention. For every broken, dusty, or dirty thing uncovered, five more items soon join my mental list even though I won't be staying long enough to take any action with it. With Mother over my shoulder, often providing her kind of directed guidance, I've managed to concentrate on the chore of dealing with the mountainous items she wants gone, which belonged to my father. Clothes. Prescribed medication. Toiletries. And a bunch of other things hiding in the various nooks and crannies.

"Yes, Mother," I agree absently.

While systematically crossing items off her list, I've found myself immersed into an unfamiliar world of a man

I didn't utter a word to in almost two decades. The menial labor of sorting and bagging items for sale, donation, or trash has had me taking inventory of my father's life and comparing it to my own. We both appeared partial to the same type of soft-bristled toothbrush and brand of sneaker, but that's where the similarities end. He preferred the order of clothes, ironed and hung, with shoes neatly paired and lined up underneath. Similarly, he had his medication and vitamins arranged in alphabetical order with each bottle well within its use-by date. My belongings fit into a few bags with washing optional, and I can't remember the last time I bothered with supplements. The stark differences speak to me of our relationship—or lack of one.

"I hope his clothes find much-needed homes and provide the new wearers joy," Mother says, referring to the bagged clothes lining the front porch, waiting for the charity pickup.

I hum in agreement, more to be polite than anything else. Time spent on these activities has kept me busy, but more importantly—to me—it has provided a crucial opportunity to think about my own life. Memories might have opened the doorway to the past, but what it's shown me is how I've grown. Clutching on to them as some sort of evidence of failure was wrong. It's clear I need to move on. Consolidate debt, get back to work, and get back to living.

It's been a productive few days on all fronts, plans formulating in my mind while elbow deep in the dust of the past. Amid each of our own emotional roller coasters, we've settled into a routine of sitting together at supper, with me heating up whatever food has been left for the day.

It has been ... okay.

Nothing more and nothing less. A portal to something better, a brighter future perhaps.

ALL FOR MOTHER

Interrupting my inner contemplations, her foot taps the tiles, and she cocks her head to the side in thought. She's going to mention retirement homes; I know it. Her so-called friends have come around to check up on her and offer their condolences, but senior living has seemed to be the topic *du jour*. These homes sound like one extended summer camp for those of the gray-haired brigade with organized outings, events, gym classes, on-site cafés, and salons. The idea itself has merit. It could break up the loneliness she now should feel. I mentally work out the weeks it would take her to have the house packed and to move, calculating how many more free days of rent I have.

"I really don't want to go into one of those assisted living places." Her lips curl, and she leans back in her chair.

If I didn't know better, I'd think she'd taken a mouthful of spoiled milk, laced with chilies. This soup, one of her neighbor's specialties—pumpkin with a hint of bacon through it—is a proven crowd-pleaser. Added herbs and vegetables give it its body and balance the flavor, but it's the smoky cured meat that provides that special *je ne sais quoi*. Based on the way she reached the bottom of her bowl, I'd say my mother liked it a lot, so I don't quite understand the sour expression.

"I thought you'd be all over that. Aren't they run like a resort?" I ask, strangely seeking her opinion on the matter.

My father was always rather vocal with his derision of the trending aged care facilities after his parents—my grandparents—moved into one. He made them sound like grazing pastures for those marching toward death and nothing more than a gossip haven for idle and bored retirees. I could understand his need to steer clear of all of that nonsense, but I thought my mother would jump on it, getting the opportunity to be the center of attention

She pauses and takes a moment to think, a wistful look to her gaze. A resort for oldies would be *my* worst nightmare. Images from the '80s sitcom *The Golden Girls* circle through my head. Harems of gray-haired biddies running around, loud and wearing ostentatious clothing ... I shudder at the thought. But for her, this would be her ideal. Or so I thought.

Frail fingers fidget with the napkin in her lap. "Maybe once, I thought it might be nice. Or good for us—Bobby and me ..." She trails off at the mention of my father, a hand finding the pewter cross hanging below her neck. It was one of the first items of jewelry he gave her early in their marriage, unable to afford the more precious metals.

They never really discussed how hard it had been in those early days, of trying to make ends meet—him on his military salary and her teaching. Growing up, when trying to work out gift ideas for her, my sister and I would always suggest a new necklace. Although others have gifted her various ones, she'd always revert back to wearing the original.

"But don't you think you'd be more comfortable in a home? There'd be people around all the time to look out for you. I thought you'd like the company, especially now." I lower my eyes, disappointed in myself for alluding to her current life status of being a widow.

Even after we've sorted and discarded some of his belongings, Father's presence is everywhere, ingrained in the fabric of the house. Images of his life captured in frames, a still reminder of who he was and how he lived. He feels very much here, a part of her life—and by default, mine at the moment.

But it's his absence that I've been noticing in her recent actions.

Her sharp intake of breath is barely audible, and her eyes meeting mine are glistening. She adjusts her hearing aids, maybe trying to tune out my insensitivity.

"I don't think so. Your father had the right idea when he bought this house." She looks away, toward the closed shutters, peering out as though they were open. "It's in a nice area, a good mix of retirees and young families. The church is really great. We've got some good fr-friends." She stutters over the last word when she realizes what she's done. She's been doing it a lot lately—using the *we* pronoun.

I'm unsure if it's the memory loss associated with her age that causes it, but she often walks into the back room that was my father's office and pauses at the door, mouth ajar, as though she's about to speak. It's a habit grown from a lifetime of his companionship—the turning around to share a funny thought, a joke, or to mention something unusual that happened that day. There's a pregnant pause when she realizes what she's done and remembers she's all alone in this house.

Well, not quite.

I'm here, but I'm a poor excuse for my father.

"It's okay, Mom," I say soothingly.

I stand and start clearing the table—something that's become routine, but right now, it's something to do in the awkwardness. Plates clink while being stacked in the dishwasher, but my hands still with the last of the cutlery when she starts speaking.

"When are you going to get married, Ash? Don't you think it's time to stop chasing your childish dreams and settle down?" Her tone has lost some of the melancholy, and I understand she's using the change of topic to stave off some of that sadness, but the new topic has the skin prickling on my arms.

My eyes close, and my jaw clenches. Of course she'd go from talking about something unsettling about herself to something she knows nothing about—voicing his opinions, his biases. It's deflection because she no longer wants to mull over her future. Maybe it's her recent thoughts of dear old dad that did it, remembering him but being vastly disappointed in only seeing me. He—for whichever of the multitude of reasons—is why I'm here.

And truth be told, he's also partially responsible for the reason I'm single and stumbling directionless through life.

"My dreams aren't childish, Mom." White knuckles slowly let go of the butter knife, and I stow it safely in with the other dirty flatware. "And it's not as though I have a choice."

She harrumphs and shakes her head, not taking stock of my words. It's a lie. She knows exactly why I don't have a family, why I never finished college. Why I'm an uneducated, failing artist. In my mind, all of that blame lies clearly with my father, and I know—*I know*—her memory isn't that bad that she's forgotten years of history. Especially since she can recall all of my sister's milestones from the same era.

While my sister is the epitome of the perfect daughter—college degree, married shortly after to a successful businessman, children—I'm the opposite. I long ago decided to leave the transgressions of the past in the past. It's hard. Those times shaped who I am as a person and where I am today. Which isn't saying much, considering my age, my single status, and that I'm currently living with my widowed mother.

My father and I, all those years ago, were once close. I remember how proud he was when he gifted me my car and I drove off to college. We had big dreams. Him influencing most of mine by directing my artistic flair in the direction of corporate America for use in the overly competitive marketing sector. It lasted until senior year when I brought my boyfriend home over the holidays with grandiose thoughts of painting full-time. For me, Brad unleashed my creativity, and he was the one I wanted—*needed*—but I still sought my parents' approval. The friction our visit caused—and the effect it had on our relationship—was the catalyst for everything that happened after.

They didn't like Brad, who he was and what he stood for. He was a bad influence in the eyes of my parents, and they couldn't look beyond that. They never wanted us together. He wasn't the match the church would endorse, and by extension, they couldn't approve either. I would've been happy to settle down with Brad, but my parents made sure that would never come to be.

Maybe they were right. Maybe he wasn't the one. But that decision—and everything that would've followed—should've been mine to make. I was under the impression that Brad had finally reached the point where he was willing to settle down. And I thought that was going to be with me. It should've been. It might've come to pass if my parents had reacted differently.

The expression on their faces when Brad and I were going to share a room on that visit …

"You had a choice," she says, alluding to the ultimatum my father gave to me. "You did then, and you do now. Your education … that boy …" She trails off, and I know exactly what she's thinking. Her nose is screwed up slightly in disgust.

She's definitely thinking about Brad and the visit during Christmas. The one where we wanted to share our love for each other with my family. The one we cut short. The one where my father pulled out the gun.

I close my eyes, not wanting to dredge up these memories and the emotions that go hand in hand with them.

"Maybe if you and Dad had let the relationship run its course instead of getting involved, it might've petered out on its own," I say through gritted teeth.

Bitter memories exist for more than one reason. Some of it is due to my parents' interference, but mainly, it's due to my uncertainty. The uncertainty of youth and young love. And the uncertainty and regret for not holding strong to my own convictions.

"Brad was a great guy and didn't deserve what you did."

"We knew there was something off with him. It was disgraceful, and you should have never been involved with him." Her tone is accusatory. The topic is a far turnaround from retirement villas and old-people resorts. She lifts her head, sucking in her cheeks, a self-satisfied smile on her lips as she continues with a conspiratorial tone, "The PI found evidence of his drinking and drug-taking as well as his more amorous activities at all the clubs."

"I knew all of this, Mom," I mutter, heat rising in my cheeks. I clutch the edge of the counter and try to control my temper.

She's doing this on purpose, trying to make me feel bad. It's the same way she tried to manipulate us as kids—by using guilt and humiliation as weapons. I remind myself that she just lost her husband and is dealing the best she can. It must be awkward, having me here, in the house, after so much time has passed. So much history.

"That sort of behavior is amoral. It had the potential to embarrass your father and his work dealings. Did you ever think about that?"

My head shakes. She only knows what she was told. After everything, I never had the decency to come home and see her while my father was alive. She'd never go behind his back, but sometimes, I wish she had. Even after enough time passed, there were too many harsh words spoken between me and him to even try to make amends. He was a prideful man and stubborn. Those traits run strong in the family.

My father was always a stickler for the rules. Being military, he had to be. It was in the fabric of his being. The issues he and I faced were a result of that, but it was also coupled with the closed-mindedness of the generation. I was seen as moving away from the more conservative ways of my upbringing and the church, but in reality, I thought I was seeing the world in all its vibrancy and political hypocrisy for the first time. Politics and religious beliefs—two things that elicit the strongest of emotions and create

ALL FOR MOTHER

the largest of obstacles. To my father, being with someone he didn't approve of made that person the poisonous snake in the garden, so he chopped off its head.

My mother bringing this up now, talking in circles about things she knows little about and shaming me, is having the desired effect. I shouldn't let it get to me, but with the ambience, smell, and lighting of the house, the scenes are vivid in my mind, as though they only happened yesterday. It's dredging up memories of self-doubt and loathing. My father had a lot to answer for ... but he's dead.

"We're family. It shouldn't have affected anything," I whisper, hearing the lie in my words.

"You knew better, Ash. Your father expected and deserved more respect than what you gave him."

And there it is. Not how embarrassed I felt when my father turned up at the college, withdrew my funding, and had the dean throw me out in my final year, months before graduation. Not how unscrupulous and dirty he made me feel for my lifestyle choices. Not how breaking up with the one man I'd promised to love forever when he proposed shattered my heart and sent me into a never-ending downward spiral. Not how I've been struggling every day to forget all of this and move on. To forgive. It's about what *I* did to him.

And this is why I waited until he was dead before I came back.

I'm not sure if I was seeking forgiveness or hoping for something more. I should've known better, and I'm thinking maybe coming here wasn't the smartest move.

FIVE

Relief washes over me as I hit Send on the acceptance e-mail for an artistic director position in Louisiana.

The laptop clicks shut, and I sigh. It's hard, starting over, and being in limbo with my mother has been like living in some sort of a time warp.

When we agreed I'd stay for a while, I thought it was the right thing to do. A way to help each other out while trying to mend a broken relationship. That's what I thought anyway. I also hoped to use the time to sort parts of my life while also being there for her, so she was not alone during the grieving process. We weren't meant to become bosom buddies. To braid each other's hair or sit around, sipping wine while discussing the latest *Jeopardy!* contestants. It was assumed we'd have our separate lives and live somewhere in the middle to meet our immediate needs.

It's become more than that. I'd suspected the aging process was in full effect, but what no one realized was how far down the path toward the end she actually was. Her mind, her mobility. She fooled us all. But I'm not the person who can be here as her crutch and help navigate the aging.

She's forgotten the conversation from last night, and the expected awkwardness at breakfast this morning is missing. It doesn't mean I've forgotten. It's weird, how her mind works, seemingly clear and focused one minute and foggy and distant the next. My body coils with tension just beneath the surface, and it's taking all of my control to maintain my patience with some of the things she's said in passing. Her passive-aggressive comments are too much, and whether she means them or not, they hurt all the same. I thought all of the biases and prejudice from the years past would be buried with my father. I just mistakenly thought that with him gone, she'd be more open and forgiving. But maybe I was giving her too much credit.

All the tasks on her list are now done. I've even taken the time to rearrange the garage, moving anything she might want down to a height where she won't need to use a ladder. She probably won't even notice.

Restless, I'm hiding in the back room, debating when I should tell her I'm leaving, and reach for an old sketchpad I found hidden in the attic across my lap. Fingers gripped around a soft-lead pencil are poised and ready for the inspiration to hit. It seems to have been sucked away along with my patience and want for being here. Across the room, my two bags lie open, topped with a kaleidoscopic mixture of soiled and clean clothes, begging to be closed and on their way. I shut the notebook and push it away in frustration.

I have no doubt Mother's and my relationship won't progress much further than where it already is. We're never going to have the same relationship she has with my sister, so I should just let it go. The conversation from last night showed that the ghostlike presence of my father is wrapped tightly around her like a dark shroud and keeps her from seeing the world outside his influence. She spent so long in Father's shadow that she doesn't want to step into the light. His opinions and life outlook are deeply ingrained in her spirit. As much as I want the opportunity to smooth things over and try to make amends for my part in our past and wish for things to be different, I'm not sure

ALL FOR MOTHER

they can be. I see the judgment. I'll always be that child who made poor choices, the one whispered about at family gatherings and behind closed doors.

My fingers tap gently on the wooden box, also found hidden in the attic. Its tarnished clasp hints at years of neglect. I have a feeling I know what I'll find when I pull open the lid, and it doesn't scare me as much as I thought it would. Mother, in a sense, already unlocked it last night.

Bronze hinges provide slight resistance, dramatically slowing the unveil. The tang of metal, oil, and gunpowder reaches my nose, confirming what I thought. Carefully, I peel back a corner of the soiled rag, concluding the final reveal.

Father's gun.

The gun that Father pulled on Brad. The gun that started and ended everything.

I lightly caress the dark steel. It's cold to the touch. Cold, just like Father's heart.

Before my thoughts wander down that sorrowful path, I assiduously wrap it back up, clicking the clasp in place with a relieved sigh. Bending, I slide it under the bed, intent on asking Mother what she wants done with it later. Hopefully, if one good thing comes out of all this, it will be me having the opportunity to dispose of the metal relic once and for all.

"Ash!"

The voice is frantic with its plea for assistance, and I roll off the bed and quickly rush out to the kitchen.

"What the—" I mutter, staring in horror at the scene unfolding.

She's not quite seated at the kitchen counter, her ass hovering above the seat as her body flails to finish the action. Pools of orange liquid, decorated with varying sizes of glass shards, lay splattered at her feet.

"Ashhhh," she groans, word low and slurred. "Help me."

Stepping around the floor-level minefield, I grab hold of her arms to steady her. Her thin and normally weak limbs involuntarily resist. I shift my weight, hoping to obtain a more secure grasp, and I attempt to position the stool with my foot behind it. If only she can sit, then I can work out what the fuck is going on.

Her exertions are causing her to hyperventilate, and she's floundering, trying to grasp the counter. These attempts abruptly stop, hands now flung to her chest and throat. I steady her and watch in horror as her eyes bulge while she struggles to get oxygen past her lips. Air trapping on the intake, she gasps, forcing it past her windpipe and into her lungs.

"My rectum," she croaks between wretched whimpers.

Her rectum? The words, if I heard them correctly, make no sense. Dizziness, anxiety, or a stroke were the things coursing through my mind, not her *rectum*.

"I'm bleeding," she says, strangling the words. "From my rectum."

I attempt to manipulate her body in a way that will allow it to sit. Her limbs aren't cooperating, and it takes all my effort to keep her standing steady. There's no blood on her clothes and none on the seat. I'm completely perplexed as to what could cause a ruptured rectum and, more importantly, why she'd think such a thing.

My body almost careens over, trying to stabilize her. She's lost the ability to control her limbs, and she becomes dead weight in my arms. I slowly attempt to lower her slack body to the ground. Gravity wins, and we land with a thud, my body cushioning her abrupt descent as best as possible. Scrambling to free our entwined bodies, I kneel at her side.

She's not breathing.

First aid lessons remembered from decades prior come to the fore. Sharp pricks pierce the underside of my palm as I move the smashed debris out of the way before rolling her somewhat onto her side. Without my support propping her, she sinks onto her back.

She's not *breathing.*

Saliva builds in my mouth, and it takes a few attempts to swallow it down. My stomach rolls, and my body trembles as I close my eyes momentarily, trying to stave off the panic.

The navy blouse rises marginally, and I stay motionless, waiting to see if I'm hallucinating or if it'll move again. There's a breath. It's somewhat labored, but it's there.

Barely.

Her pallor changes to almost translucent, and my fingers rub against the papery skin on her wrist, searching for a pulse. I try to situate myself, and my knee jostles her somewhat, prompting her head to loll to the side. Blue-tinged lips part, showcasing yellowed teeth through a slack jaw.

She's a corpse.

It's my turn to stop breathing as I frantically search for the imperceptible, weak pump of blood underneath her skin. Her eyes are vacant, unnervingly staring through me ...

There is no pul—

There it is! Maybe? It's hard to tell, my slick and quivering fingers not able to maintain the pressure needed without taking a hard hold.

"Ash? Wh-what happened?" Scarcely audible words pass through a locked jaw, and eyelids flutter.

Air I didn't realize I had been holding is expelled slowly. I didn't kill her. For those few minutes—which felt like all the time and no time at all—I thought I had.

Sweat beads on my brow as I press buttons on the home phone, only leaving her side for a fraction of a second to collect it.

"Nine-one-one. What's your emergency?"

"It's my mother …" My eyes move toward the ceiling as I struggle to find the words. Stumbling through an explanation, I then follow the dispatcher's directions for a variety of tests to help assess my mother's condition.

The color hasn't returned, and she still looks like a corpse. Her eyes remain distant, now blinking slowly. Mouth opening and closing slightly like a rusty hinge. I gently place one of the decorative sofa cushions under her head. Her pallid complexion pinkens a little, and her eyes blink with combined confusion and fear.

She almost died.

Remaining on the line while waiting for an ambulance, I close my eyes and nod in acknowledgment to the dispatcher's continued gentle probing, forgetting until prompted that my nonverbal cues are useless. His calm voice continues to offer support and keeps me grounded.

She could've died.

My hand searches for her, and with water tearing my eyes, I whisper comforting words, telling her to hold on and that help is coming. Her shaky, shallow breaths break my heart.

"It's going to be okay, Mom," I say, stroking the sallow skin on her face. "I'm here. Help's on its way."

At my words of reassurance, her head tilts to some degree toward me, and she smiles. "I miss Bobby," she manages to say. "I miss him so much. It'd be so peaceful if I could join him."

Tears stream down my face. Her words break me.

In this moment, years of feud-filled tension evaporate as I try to convey my love and forgiveness with a look. With a touch.

I know she misses her husband. I've seen the times when she forgets and then has to remember he's gone all over again. Whatever the differences between me and my father and for all of Mother's annoying little traits and OCD-like tendencies, I can't negate the love she shared with him. Their love was one I used to aspire to. It was the old style of love. The once-in-a-lifetime connection between two people, unmarred by the changing times and new societal norms. A devotion that truly upheld the *death do us part* vow. He was the Fred Astaire to her Ginger Rogers, a black-and-white romance with cheesy one-liners, flowing skirts, and the unhealthy obsession to turn life into a cheerful song and dance. But he was also the family's mortar, and his absence has resulted in foundational cracks and crumbling in the previously seamless brickwork. He was her *raison d'être*, so I understand how her soul must be urging her to let go.

My mouth quivers, managing to hold back a sob. Eyes closing to suppress the tears, I ignore the questions being spoken in my ear and voice my fear, "Don't leave me, Mom."

When faced with the mortality of this woman, all of the little niggles and annoyances flee my mind. They are small and inconsequential. How we allow such trivial and nonsensical bullshit to cloud our perception and get under our skin, I honestly can't comprehend right now.

"Don't die," I beg, voice cracking. "Please don't die. Not today."

The ambulance arrives, and its staff comes in, poking and prodding appendages with various machines. They're worried. But I'm no longer concerned. If anything, I'm now confused. She's more than okay; I can tell because she's started *prodding* them for their life story and *poking* around to find some personal connection. It's incessant; she won't shut up. In total busybody nirvana, she collects tidbits to possibly pass on at her next card game gossip session. Connecting the dots to see who they're all related to, schools they went to, children they might have, and how they fit into the scheme of the town and things.

She's not dying. She's been resurrected, and I feel the fraud.

I look to the marble counter—where minutes before, she was teetering on the edge—and I realize that if I hadn't been there, it would've been the end for her. Her head would've struck the corner on her way down. If I had been out or not even here at all, she would've lain there helpless, unconscious and bleeding until someone found her. And that could have been days.

She'd be dead.

"Lucky you were here with her," the overweight medic says, mirroring my thoughts, after hitching his radio receiver onto his belt.

I nod.

"We're going to take her to the hospital to run some tests. Find out what brought on the dizziness and get an X-ray. She might have sustained a break or a fracture from the fall."

"What?" I say, moving my attention from him to my mother.

"It might not be. It could be just a sprain," he says with a shrug. "There's swelling, but generally, when aged patients fall, we find it's a break. Their bones are too brittle, and it doesn't take much."

"Oh," is all I can say.

He doesn't seem too bothered by it, so I try not to overthink my part in this unfolding saga, where I could be the one responsible for breaking her leg. Bones like twigs—that's what they'd have to be like to snap on impact. I didn't even think she'd hit the floor with any force. I thought I'd stopped that.

"I tried to lay her down gently ... I did," I finally say, running my hands through my hair. "It's my fault if it's broken. She's going to hate being on crutches."

The laugh is boisterous, and I look over at him, confused, anger swelling with his impropriety. My mother could have died. And I might have broken her leg. He sees something on my face that reins in his response.

"Sorry." He raises his hands, palms facing outward, but is unable to hide the humor on his lips. "It's unlikely she'll get crutches. They're too hard for the elderly—the balancing and the coordination, not to mention pinching under the arms. She'll more than likely be wheelchair-bound or reliant on a wheeled walker."

Wheelchair? Shit.

I scratch my head and look around on wobbly legs. Grasping the chair, I watch as they carefully place her onto the gurney and secure the straps. Color has returned to her skin; it now has a more normal glow rather than the deathly ash gray. Her lips are moving a million miles per hour, but I don't hear whatever nonsense she's sharing with the paramedics as they pull a blanket up over her.

The chair squeaks as I finally sit, leaving them to their task and to her. I exhale slowly as the heels of my palms dig into my eyes sockets before dragging them down my face. I've just lived an eternity in the space of an hour.

"There's no need for you to ride in the ambulance with us unless you want to," the medic says, ambling over, invading my quiet space. He now carries the clipboard with the notes on my mother's condition and has lost the joviality from before. "Her vitals are fine, and the ride back to the hospital will be a routine one. You can meet us there, if you'd like."

"Okay." Elbows resting on the counter, I wipe the moisture from my forehead and think.

"Ash? Ash!"

Everyone's staring at me, seemingly waiting for a response of some sort. Her brows knit together into a crinkled frown, and it's as though I were a teenager again.

"Sorry, Mother. What did you say?"

"We're leaving now," the medic speaks before she gets the chance to answer, and annoyance flashes over her face.

"Yes," she agrees, pursing her lips at him before directing her attention back to me. "I'll see you at the hospital."

I nod and watch them leave.

After all the commotion and excitement, the room is now silent. It seeps under my skin, and I'm left feeling bereft. A wave of sadness laps at my extremities, disheartening me. The house is empty, despondent, just like me.

My limbs are sluggish as I sweep up the broken glass to dispose of it in the trash. The orange juice has long since dried on the tiles, and I use a wet cloth to scrub away the spillage.

Morbid thoughts make me wonder, *If I hadn't been here or if I had ignored her, would it be blood staining the floor?*

She could have died.

Mother's bones must be like fine china—shiny, aged, and shattering apart when dropped. She's not going to be happy, returning home, incapacitated. At least she'll be utilizing a walking aid. She'll be forced to. It won't be congenial or convenient, but hopefully, it'll be the transition she needs to realize that mobility aids are a necessity.

I stand and put everything away in its right place. When they're wiped clean, it's as though Mother's fall never happened. I wish I could push away the memory of her cadaverous body when I thought she was dead from my mind just as easily.

On autopilot, I change, gather the items I think Mother might need, and leave for the hospital.

SIX

The overhead fluorescent lights are overly bright, its luminescence bouncing off the walls and floor. My hand tightens on the leather straps of the bag holding Mother's change of clothes as I follow the directions provided by the lady at reception.

I hear the laughter and allow myself to be guided by their voices rather than counting off bed numbers. The privacy curtains are pulled around the cubicle, where my mother's voice is coming from, and I stand outside for a moment, determining if it's safe to enter. I'm about to announce my presence when the metal rings are hastily pulled to the side. The nurse jumps back, startled, before giggling.

"You have a visitor." Her name tag identifies her as Josie, and her smile widens as she looks over my shoulder. "Two it seems."

There's a soft chuckle from behind me, and I turn to see who has brightened the nurse's day. His scrubs are a different color to those worn by staff I've seen in the hospital. A brown leather messenger bag strapped across his body cements my thoughts that he mustn't work here.

"Hi, I'm Joel. From Dr. Fredericks's office," he says, stepping around me. "I've brought over the moon boot to fit you. If that's okay, Mrs. Doyle."

He shuffles further into the hospital bay and stands in front of Mother. She's preening with all the attention focused on her. Ignoring me, she listens intently to Joel as he explains how the boot will help keep her leg stabilized and still allow her to walk around freely. Josie flitters in and out, answering questions when asked and checking the monitors even though it doesn't look like Mother is attached to anything.

"How long will she need to be in the boot?" My question has them all turning toward me as if I were an intruder.

"This is my Ash," Mother says simply. "My husband recently passed, and Ash has been keeping me company and helping me sort through some of his belongings."

"That's so thoughtful," Joel says, lifting Mother's leg and gently placing it within the confines of the boot. He looks up and offers a grin before securing the Velcro straps. "Now, Dr. Fredericks reviewed the X-rays and thought you'd respond well with the boot. If there are no complications, the bones should mend fully in three months."

Mother's lips purse slightly, and I can see she's going to have an opinion on wearing such ugly accoutrement for that extended period.

Joel must feel the shift in her mood and continues on brightly, "We could've done a splintered plaster cast, but they can get annoying. Itchy and smelly." His nose scrunches up in faux distaste. "At least, with the boot, you'll be able to take it off to change your socks and to shower."

Mother blinks slowly.

"You don't want a plaster cast," Nurse Smiley says from the side. "These new moon boots are so much better. And easier as well." She shoots Joel a coy look, licking her lips as he continues the fitting.

ALL FOR MOTHER

"My, my." Mother's back to being perky and back to ignoring me. "I feel like a princess with both of you being so attentive and helpful."

She watches as they fuss around her. I try to recall her being overly flirty like this with people when I was a kid, but I can't think of any examples that go beyond the standard expected politeness. Her over-the-top interaction is something I've noticed when we've been out or there's been visitors to the house. It's like she has been starved for attention and endeavors to make up for it with everyone but me. She soaks it up and tries to wring every last morsel of conversation from them.

They don't realize it's fake, a forced nice-grandma persona put on just for them, sucking all of her energy and good disposition. My superpower of reading her moods started at childhood, and now, as an adult, through awakened eyes, I see so much more of the subtle manipulation and exaggeration she employs on people around her. I'm tuned in so finely that I'm able to foresee exactly when the facade will drop as she bottoms out to normal. I'm lucky. I just get the real Mother.

"There you go. All done." Joel steps back, admiring his handiwork as her leg hangs limply over the side of the bed.

"The doctor said we could discharge you once the boot was fitted, so I'll get the paperwork finalized and help you into the wheelchair," Josie says.

"B-but—" Mother starts to speak at the same time I hold up the bag with her clothes.

Josie nods in understanding, taking it from me. "Let's get you changed first," she says, closing the privacy curtain.

While they're secreted away again behind the partition, Joel comes and stands beside me. He pulls a few items from his bag and holds them out.

"Can I have a quick word, if you don't mind?"

At his direction, I follow him a few steps out of the nurse's and Mother's hearing, and he explains some of the care instructions for the boot and goes through the issues that she might have with it. Blisters. Secondary site pain. The spongy foam squares he gives me are extra padding to cushion any pressure sores. There's a whole lot of medical jargon, basically translating to Mother needing more care, which has me sinking in despair.

"Will you stay with your mom for a while?" he asks after finally exhausting the rundown of everything moon boot–related.

I shuffle my feet, arms crossed, hugging my torso. It's a loaded question.

"Not for much longer. I have a job lined up in New Orleans that's starting next week."

There's laughter coming from Mother's cubicle, and we both look over to see the area open and Josie helping her into the wheelchair.

"I haven't told her about it yet."

Joel hums and strokes his closely trimmed beard in thought. "It'd be rather difficult for her to live on her own. Is there another relative who can take over for you when you leave? Or is the family in a position to move her to assisted living, even for a short stay?"

"Three months seems rather long for her to be in that boot. Don't bones mend faster than that?" I ask, trying to remember how long kids wore their casts when we were in school. "It's just a fracture. Aren't they meant to take six weeks?"

"Double fracture. And maybe, if she were younger." He reaches out and squeezes my arm. "Bones in the elderly take much longer to heal. She'll be lucky if she's out of the boot in three months; it'll more likely be six."

"Six months," I repeat incredulously.

I went through scenarios in my mind while driving to the hospital, wondering what level of care would be needed if she had broken her leg. Worst case, I thought she could stay with Bel, but there's no way she will want to stay with her for up to six months, or vice versa. Nor is there any way I can see her agreeing to move into a hospice-type situation for that time frame. Not when she has the house. I wonder if home care would be a viable solution. Unless she finally sells and moves into an aged care facility. So many possibilities and none really that can be decided on and put into action overnight.

"I suppose I'll have to stay until we can sort it all out. Go through our options." My chin lowers to my chest as I take a few deliberate breaths. "Are you sure it'll take that long for the break to heal?"

Joel nods.

Shit.

"Oh well. There's nothing we can do about it, I suppose," I mutter.

Joel and I stand in comfortable silence, watching Josie fuss over my mother. When he speaks, his words are kind and thoughtful. "What you are doing—have been doing—is so considerate. You don't see that much anymore—kids taking the time to look after and help their parents. Normally, they're happy to ship them straight off into assisted living or some form of a retirement home and have someone else take on that burden. Good for you."

My chest swells the same time my cheeks heat from his words. It was my intent to help her. To be there for her. But it's hard. The more I'm around her, the more I find she's not the same person from my youth—or maybe she is, and I was just blind to it. But time and circumstance have definitely changed her into this forgetful and sometimes-bitter person.

"It's hard though," Joel continues, as if reading my thoughts. "And it will only get harder. She's going to need help, more than normal, to do the everyday stuff."

My eyes quickly dart up to him.

"Here," he says after a hesitant pause, retrieving a business card and hurriedly scribbling something on it before handing it to me. "These are my numbers—work and personal—in case you want to talk anything over. I know how hard this will be for both of you, and if you need help or advice, all you need to do is ask."

With a small nod, he turns and strides down the hallway toward the elevators. By the time he's rounded the corner and out of sight, Josie and Mother have joined me.

"Your mother's all ready to go home now. She might need some more pain relief in a few hours. It's up to her whether she manages it with the scripted Panadeine Forte or over-the-counter relief." This is said for my benefit as Josie hands over some discharge notes, including a hospital printout with instructions on how to manage pain. She bends down next to the wheelchair, at eye-level with Mother. "It was a pleasure meeting you, Mrs. Doyle. You take care of yourself."

With that, we're dismissed, and I take over, wheeling Mother in the direction Joel just went, with a heavy heart and a clouded mind. Mother talks the whole way out to the car, criticizing this or that. How Josie and Joel would make a cute couple, even naming their babies. And how Josie's hoping to get Joel's number. I feel the weight of those digits in my pocket, smile, and drown out the rest of the one-sided conversation.

SEVEN

The hospital faxed the scripts to Mother's pharmacy, and I am more than thankful it has a drive-through for us to pick up the medication. The high she was on while Joel and Josie fussed over her has long since subsided. She's silent ... and maybe a bit sullen, but she's in no way quiet. Her actions are acutely loud.

There was the sharp intake of breath when I cleared the speed bumps from the hospital parking lot. The gasp during the right turn at the set of lights as she was swept toward the door. A little mewl at the Stop sign. She might not have spoken since we left—which was a feat in itself and an indicator for something bigger—but I sensed her pain and frustration with every mile through every whimper.

The timing of her fall and subsequent break couldn't be further from ideal. For the first time in what felt like an eternity, I thought I was climbing out of the hole. Work was lined up, and I was actually excited at the possibility of it. Some of that eagerness could well have been my growing desire to get out of Mother's house. Too many memories were churning up the past, but at least they gave me the clarity to try to accept them and move on.

With a thud, my head hits the back of the seat, and I exhale loudly, waiting for the color of the light to change.

The *click, click, click* of the indicator echoes loudly in the confined space.

Bel will have to step in to look after Mother. There's no way I should be expected to stay on to do it.

A quick glance in Mother's direction has me feeling guilty for my internal musings. She's so frail. So fragile. It's hard to quell the anger of the past, and I know it's coming from my own selfishness, brought on by years of emotional abuse and self-sabotage.

And here I was, thinking I was finding peace with it all.

I still the thoughts of Mother and this now-emerging situation with her care and well-being. The complexity of it is uncomfortable.

Joel. His number burns a hole in my pocket, and I smile, remembering the sparkle disappearing from Josie's demeanor when she realized he'd left while she was dealing with Mother.

It's probably nothing.

Probably no more than the willingness to provide direction with any arising issues due to Mother and her leg, per his words. He was good-looking, and one can always dream. Maybe if I thought there was more—or the potential for more—in the look we shared, I'd consider starting something. Call him up, hoping for a date. One can only wish. But such notions are ridiculous, and me reading too much into situations like this was the catalyst behind most of my impetuous decisions in the past. I swore to turn over a new leaf. To start anew.

My arguments and concerns keep me company on the drive through the estate.

"Are you okay, Mom?" I ask, pulling slowly into the driveway of her house.

"What, hon?" Dazed, rapidly blinking eyes search the surroundings, as though she's not sure of where she is.

"Do you think you'll be okay to get inside?" I look through the windshield to the front porch. There's no way

I'll be able to carry her up there. And then there's the issue of the rotting wood on two of the steps, which I have yet to find someone to fix. It's not safe.

Her laugh is short and followed with a pained groan.

"No, Ash," she says. "Of course I'm not okay. This … this boot's so tight. The weight of it, it's so heavy, and it's already hurting my knee."

She gingerly clutches her knee, cradling it as though it were a baby bird who'd just fallen from the nest and broken its wing.

"I don't understand how the doctor believes I can walk on it. I can barely lift it, and I'm sitting."

The black plastic surrounding half of her lower leg pretty much glares at me, taunting untold promises I'm sure to hate. Pressing the coded button on the visor, I open the garage door. The number of steps inside, ascending into the kitchen, are just the same, but at least there's no rot, and the space between the wall and banister is minimal.

"It's okay, Mom. We'll work it out."

My words are soft, an attempt to sound soothing. I exit the car with a sigh and run a hand through my hair while wondering how I'm going to make truth from my words. The contents of the garage goad me, and it takes a moment before I spy the wheeled walker in the corner. It was Father's, apparently. He needed it in his final weeks, unable to walk unassisted. Mother will be needing it over the coming months and probably beyond, but for now, I'm confident I can use it in the place of a wheelchair.

Wheels squeak as it's rolled to the passenger door, and I position it in a way I think could work. Crouching down beside her, I take her hand in mine, watching as her shoulders shudder and tears glisten under the soft glow of the car's internal light.

"Mom, I'm going to lift your legs and move them around here, so they're outside of the car," I say gently, as though speaking to a small, frightened child. "Can you help me with that? I don't want to hurt you, so you'll need to turn your body outward as well. Okay?"

A fresh sob breaks free as she answers, "I don't know if I can, Ash. It hurts."

"I know, Mom. But we have to try. You can't stay out here all night." I smile, wiping the moisture away from under her eyes. "Are you ready?"

She nods, and I carefully lift her feet and swing them around until they're out of the vehicle. The boot is awkward. So large and bulky compared to her scrawny legs, and I can see how it's causing her discomfort.

"I'm going to need you to stand, so I can help you sit on Father's walker. We'll use it like a wheelchair. Okay?"

"Okay," she whispers, lifting her arms for me to help her.

When she stands, her head hits the doorframe, eliciting an instant, painful cry. The height of the boot has her off-balance, and she almost immediately topples to the side. I steady her, but her light frame has the weight and awkwardness of a baby elephant, jerking and working against me as I desperately try to maneuver her where I want her.

She's finally seated, and I take a deep breath of relief. The stairs are the next hurdle, and I close my eyes, not looking forward to the effort it's going to take to get her up them and into the house. This is going to be so much harder than it looks. And much more painful. I briefly wonder why they never installed a stairlift, one of those electronically operated chairs that transports a person up and down. It confounds me. Mother's mobility and balance are compromised at best, and I can't imagine how Father must have been in his last days.

"Come, Mother. Let's get you inside and into bed," I say with false positivity. "Everything will be better in the morning after a good night's rest."

EIGHT

"*Everything will be better in the morning.*"

Famous last words.

Nothing is better. Nothing at all.

"Why can't you take her?" I'm wearing a path in the carpet with the pacing. My call to Bel this morning has been nothing but frustrating, and I can't help the whining tone in my voice. "I have a job lined up. I can't stay."

"Isn't it convenient, after years of acting the desolate, unemployed drifter, you suddenly have responsibilities?" The tinny echo across the phone line distorts Bel's laugh, giving it a sinister quality. "Not this time, Ash. You wanted back into the family, so it's your turn to step up and deal with it."

"That's not fair. What do you think I've been doing the past week?" I take a seat on the bed, slumping over and picking at the frayed edge of the bedspread. "I'm all packed. If Mother hadn't fallen, I'd have told her today. It's your turn. What's your excuse?"

"I have a job and a family. I don't have the time."

"How long do you think it will take to organize for a home nurse or something?" I scour my mind for all the little snippets of relevant information I've managed to pick up over the past week from Mother and her visitors. The ones who discussed retirement homes, caregivers, and the like. "Or a room in one of those assisted living places?"

Bel's silent on the other end of the phone.

"Mom's been talking about moving into one of these facilities," I say. "Can't we just speed the timeline up or something?"

"We can't," she says softly. "There's no money."

"What? That's ridiculous." In the time I've been here, there's been no indication that Mother didn't have any money. As far as I'm aware, she still gets her teaching pension, and Father's military pension should have transferred over to her.

"We've been going through all the books. They're a total mess. But there's nothing, just debt. She has the house, and we're looking to settle the outstanding note on it after we pay off everything else when Dad's life insurance comes through. She has her pension, and that's it."

What?

Mother's car is a newer model, upgraded in the last twelve months. Her wardrobe holds recent purchases. Framed photos around the house display evidence of vacations with Father and friends. The medical expenses for Father's illness would have been covered by their insurance. She provides a substantial weekly tithe to the church. There's been no overt evidence of them having money issues.

"Does she know?"

"No," she says. "And I'm not planning on telling her until we finalize everything. She can't move, and I don't think hiring someone to care for her is financially prudent."

"What about her health insurance? Won't that cover some sort of in-home care?" Surely, this is the sort of thing it's designed to provide.

"It might have if all the payments had been kept current. There'd still be a substantial copay." She sighs. "I can make a few calls—and I will because all this needs to be sorted. But it takes time. For now, it's probably best if we keep her care in the family, and I can't do it. It would help so much if you would."

Maybe she's right, but as much as I wish I could be the person to step up and take charge to help Mother get through this, I don't think I can. The concept of family obligation is foreign to me. There's been too many years of estrangement, having only myself to worry about. I know myself and recognize that undertaking a task like this could mentally bury me. I don't want to be trapped. On one hand, there's a part of me that wants to jump in a hundred and ten percent just to prove I can, but on the other I want to run as fast as I can, a continuation of my forced escape decades prior.

"But I don't want to," I say, whispering the truth to both hands.

"Ash, I believe in you. You can do this. I've got to go now and get the kids ready for school. Bye."

The phone's silent in my hand, displaying nothing but a locked screen. Bel's left me to deliberate alone, and I'm unsure of what to do. I know what I want to do. I want to hide until all of this messiness ends. I'm not a nursemaid, and helping Mother last night was the extent of how comfortable I am with doing this. I want to make good on the promises I made to do better, be better, so I can move forward. I want to get on with my life, as a responsible grown-up, but I don't think me staying here is the right decision. I have a new job to think about. I just want to bury all of this in the past and with Father.

It's too early, and I'm tired. Sleep last night was hard-won. Turbulent thoughts warred, and I was on edge, worried I'd miss Mother calling out for me. Cold water splashed on my face does little for my alertness, and I pull a sweater on before heading to her room. If I'm hungry, she should be as well.

I pause at her door, listening for any indication that she's awake before quietly pushing it open.

"What the—"

It's unclear whether she's struggling to sit or roll over. Tangled bedsheets are caught around the large lump of plastic at the end of her leg, and the more she tries to move, the more they appear to constrict their hold.

I pull my shoulders back and enter the room on a mission. "Here, Mom. Let me help."

The bedding takes a minute to unravel before I'm able to move her into a sitting position.

"I'm sorry, Ash. I'm so sorry."

She looks away, cheeks flushed and ears turning red. I place a hand under her arm, supporting her to stand, pretending not to see or feel the wetness of the sheets.

"It's no bother. Let's get you up and dressed."

We move into the bathroom, and I peel off her clothes, warming a washcloth to clean her. It's becoming more obvious that she'll need a lot of assistance in the short-term, until she gets back some of her mobility. I wish I could laugh at the irony that it's me who's here, but there's no humor in this situation; it's saddening. Even more so as the layers of her current circumstances slowly unravel.

"Is Bel coming to look after me for a while, or will you be staying?"

Seeing her floundering highlighted her frailty and sparked a level of compassion deep in my bones. It makes it difficult to make a decision on whether I should stay. I don't want to help even though I have this instinct to want to. I don't want to be the one nursing her back to health, but I also don't know what else can be done.

"I'm not sure, Mom. We'll work it out."

I'm not sure how. She has no one other than us, and apparently, she has nothing other than the roof over her head. Her whole life has led to this point—alone, desolate, and at the total mercy of others—and she doesn't even know it.

And I am here.

Family.

ALL FOR MOTHER

But is it enough?

Uncle John's words from the funeral come back, unbidden.

"Don't screw this up."

NINE

"You'll also need an over toilet aid if you don't have one," Joel says, chewing on a straw.

My cheeks ache from the forced tight smile as I scribble down what I hope to be the last item in my notepad. Sharing a coffee with Joel has been pleasant even though I wish it were under different circumstances. Hunched in a corner of the Starbucks at Kroger, straddling two estates cut by the interstate, is probably not what he was thinking when he suggested a meetup. Unfortunately, it was the only place I could get to relatively easily without being away from the house for a huge period of time while ticking off the need for groceries.

The list we're compiling is for items needed to help Mother negotiate her temporary disability. Things she probably should've already had in the house to assist with her and Father's declining health and mobility.

"What is that?" I ask, dropping the pen on the table to pick up and take a sip of my lukewarm coffee.

This has been such an education. There's so much stuff I didn't know existed that is needed or used by people, let alone my mother.

He laughs, the deep chortling sound comforting. I roll my shoulder, releasing some of the tension that's been increasing since this morning. He makes it all sound so simple. So straightforward. It gives me hope that it's not going to be as monumentally hard as I built it up in my mind.

His eyes hold the same kindness I noticed the night at the hospital. "It's a plastic toilet seat in a frame, which you position over the existing ceramic toilet. You can raise it to a height that'll assist your mom with sitting and standing without help."

"That's going to the top of the list."

He pulls the pad over in front of him, perusing the items. Picking up the pen, he scratches some more notes and copies something from his phone.

"I wrote down the name and number of a local disability shop. They'll have all of these items, and they might be able to suggest some others as you need them."

"Thanks so much for taking the time for this." I run my fingers through my hair and lean back to rest my head against the wall. I'm so tired. If I closed my eyes now, I know I'd drift off. "I had no idea getting old could be so messy. Or difficult."

Joel smiles gently and reaches across the table, taking my hand in his. "It can be. It can also be extremely rewarding. Once you get a few of these things to help make the everyday tasks easier, you'll get into a routine. Caring for the elderly takes a special kind of commitment, and your concern and dedication to your mother are impressive."

His words wash over me like the tendrils of a late summer breeze, showering me in warmth and sunlight. It's a similar compliment to one he's given before, and it's the one I desperately needed to hear today.

The day has been very long and frustrating for both Mother and me as we navigated the new living arrangements. Trying to establish what worked and what didn't took time and a lot of patience on my part. Taking on the role of her caregiver is not the position I want to be in. I don't think I'd do it if she were functioning in an almost-independent way. After today, both of our emotions are on a short fuse.

"I'm only trying to do what needs to be done. Anyone would do the same for their mother." I blink, realizing for the first time that I sound like my mother, spouting off some politically correct and overly polite response. Words said because they're expected since no one wants to hear or be judged by the reality.

"No, Ash. You're wrong. Most lack the inherent compassion it takes to care for an older relative," he says, giving my hand a quick squeeze. "That's why aged care is such a booming business. Are you considering any assisted living arrangements?"

I lie and shake my head. Of course we thought about it. I've been thinking about it almost nonstop since my conversation with Bel. But it's not an option. Not yet anyway.

"After my father's death, everything's been upside down. I don't think she's willing to leave the memories of the house yet." I shrug, not knowing what else to say.

"When are you leaving for Louisiana?"

"My job in New Orleans?" I rub my eyes and swallow. "I'm not sure. They were very understanding and said they'd hold the position for a few weeks. But the family's still sorting through the estate on Mom's behalf, and I don't think it'll be resolved by then."

"Death is messy. Almost as messy as life." He withdraws his hand from mine, twisting his arm to look at his watch. "It's time I got back to the clinic. I've still got a few hours left on my shift."

"Of course." There's an awkward moment when we both stand. I look down to my worn trainers, fidgeting with the strap on my bag. "Thanks again for meeting with me. I really appreciate the advice."

He moves in closer and places a kiss on my cheek before stepping back. It happens in a fraction of a moment, but the rough stubble of his facial hair scrapes an awareness across my skin that travels down to the extremities of my body.

"I'll see you later."

He turns, and with a flutter in my belly, I watch as he walks out of the building and into the parking lot. With a grin, I amble into the store and drift off into my own thoughts while placing grocery items into the cart. Humming a simple tune, I tell myself that everything will be all right, and for once, I let myself believe it.

"I don't need this stuff. What do I want it for?"

Mother flicks the piece of paper and turns her head away. With quick reflexes, I manage to catch it before it hits the floor.

"It'll make everything easier. The doctor said you need to be walking around," I say, sitting on the edge of one of the chairs in her sunroom.

The shutters are closed but twisted in the direction that allows light to filter through. I'd open them, but …

"I can't be wheeling you everywhere, and I can't be here at your beck and call to either carry you or push you."

"It hurts too much. I can't walk."

The slow movement of the chair as it reclines and raises the leg rest takes away from her tantrum. It's hard to see her point when she throws her body back into the chair, and if I wasn't so frustrated right now, I'd laugh at her.

"I get that; I do. But if you don't use the muscles, you might never be able to walk again."

She opens one glaring eye as her lips harden into a thin line, crinkling the wrinkles surrounding it. "So, you're a specialist now? And where did you get your medical degree from, hmm?"

My eyes blink slowly with a deep inhalation.

ALL FOR MOTHER

One one thousand. Two one thousand. Three …

Harsh words are held back by a clenched jaw, allowing their vitriol to be diluted.

"The boot's too heavy; it's too hard to walk," she whines softly. "I can barely lift it, and you expect me to drag it around the house. Thought you were here to help me, not torture me."

I sigh. "Mom, the doctor said—"

"Yes, I know what he said. I was there too. Stop treating me like a child," she snaps.

"But, Mom …" I take a deep breath and center myself. Allowing the anger that's gradually building out is not going to achieve anything. I know it's hard for her to accept this level of help from anyone. It must be like a slap in the face—and probably doubly so because I'm the one here helping her and not her favorite daughter. "This stuff will help. I met with Joel—one of the staff from Dr. Fredericks's office—and he recommended all of this."

"Joel? Is that where you were this afternoon?" Her demeanor changes as she filters through her memory, searching for him. I see the moment it registers, and she looks at me shrewdly, eyebrows narrowing. "Was he that delightful boy who brought the boot to the hospital?"

"Yes," I say.

"Oh, he was so nice. He knew what he was doing when he fitted this wretched thing. I can forgive him though because he was so good-looking. He and nurse Josie would make a cute couple. Don't you think, Ash?"

"Huh?"

The way her brain works—jumping from subject to subject, shifting her mood from one extreme to another—is confusing. I didn't realize her mind had become so scattered until after being forced into her presence for almost every minute of it today. It takes me a beat to follow the conversation the way she's dictated it.

Of course she'd be up to playing matchmaker to two complete strangers, not even considering a cute guy would be a match for me.

"Joel and Josie. Sounds cute too."

"Mom, I don't think—"

"So, when are you going to get these things, so I can start walking around and doing stuff for myself?" she says, cutting me off and changing the subject again.

My head's spinning, trying to grasp her logic, and it takes me a second to understand that she has done a complete one-eighty and is now wanting these items she was so vehemently resisting not a few minutes ago. If I'd known Joel's name held the power to make her amenable, I would have led with it. At this point, I decide not to dwell on the fact that it took the mention of him to convince her, that my words weren't enough. If it takes a village to raise a child, then it appears that it takes a different one to aid the elderly. Regardless, I'm taking it as a win.

"I've spoken to the store, and they've everything in stock. If I order tonight, we can have it delivered tomorrow."

There's a brief moment of silence as we consider each other.

"Okay," she says, looking away and muttering to herself. "Okay."

I inwardly cheer and take my leave before she can change her mind.

TEN

She can't bathe herself.
Fuck my life.

How she hasn't slipped or fallen before now confounds me. I never put much thought into how she'd been washing or how dangerous wet tiles could be. I never realized how long it had taken her before she broke her leg. She'd just disappear and then come back sometime later, freshly cleaned and changed. Why would I think of these things? Who wants to know the details or imagine their mother showering?

How on earth did she and Father manage in those months or weeks leading up to his death?

She has a shower chair—a plastic white stool—in the glass enclosure. As far as I can tell, it's been used to hold the body and face wash. When I was previously in her bathroom, disposing of Father's toiletries, I thought it was a shelf for shower items. There are no grab bars.

According to one of Mother's long-winded stories, an occupational therapist surveyed the house when Father's health started to decline, and she suggested a lot of these things, including the grab bars. At the time of the OT's visit to assess the living arrangements, Mother was ambulant and able to balance for periods of time without the use of an aid. She and my father refused to listen to the OT's advice and make any changes. It was the vanity talking. Stubbornness too. Maybe even a bit of pride. But it's too late now. She'll have to wait until the insurance payout to get them to be installed now.

If only they had listened.

"Ash! Make sure the water's running hot." Mother's voice echoes off the bathroom's ceramic-covered walls, an effort since she's currently seated in the sunroom at the back of the house. "I don't want to catch a chill."

My fingernails dig into the stack of plush towels held in my arms as I fantasize about shredding them apart and coating the room with torn fragments of purple Egyptian cotton. The tantrum would serve no purpose. It would only feel better for a moment, and I'd still have to deal with Mother. The prodding and poking only encourage retaliation with more prodding and poking. It's best to remain calm. Be an adult.

I'm not a child. I'm not a child. I am not a child. I take a deep breath and hold it, eyes closed with cheeks puffed out, repeating my mantra with as much conviction as I can muster before exhaling.

"Yes, Mother."

Slowly, I set about preparing the room for her shower. I'm trying to follow the advice I read online and have everything laid out and ready. Once I get her into the cubicle, I don't think I can leave her to grab any forgotten items. I know she's looking forward to being clean, the quick bird-bath washes from yesterday and this morning not really the same. I know the intimacy involved is going to be uncomfortable for the both of us. My head has already ended up between her legs a few times today when I was placing her feet through her incontinence pant leg holes. If I keep it as clinical as possible, then hopefully, I won't need to see or touch anything more than necessary.

I let the silver snake-like shower hose fall to the cubicle floor before turning on the hot water and busying myself in the room. The old pipes rattle in distress, showing their age and voicing their opposition before water juts out, only to angrily gurgle down the drain. Four towels are on the adjacent basin, half on standby to mop up any water if required. I'll use one on the floor, one for her chair, and the other for her to dry herself. The last one will be held in reserve, just in case.

"Okay. You've got this," I mutter to myself while doing a final survey of the room to make sure everything's ready.

It's a risk, having the water on before she's seated, but I'd rather feel her rubbery, naked skin as I help her in than the wrath from the water being cold.

"You took your time. I thought we'd be done by now." She struggles to stand as I hover closely, waiting for her to turn and sit on the wheeled walker. "I don't want to miss the start of the Lifetime midday movie."

"We've got plenty of time," I say, disengaging the brakes and pushing her into the bedroom.

"Did you leave the water on?" She tsk-tsks, craning her head to the side, ear in the direction of the bathroom. "Are you wasting all the hot water?"

"No, Mother."

She settles on the edge of the bed, and I unfasten the boot and remove her socks. Ensuring the brakes are engaged on the walker, I position it in front of her and leave her to finish undressing to turn the water off. She'll keep complaining until I do. A cursory check finds everything as I left it.

She's partially unclothed and waiting when I return, sitting in her diaper and shirt. Beside her, the discarded garments have been haphazardly folded in a pile with the skill of a five-year-old. By rote, I dump them into the laundry basket and pull out a fresh nightgown. Her chattering teeth remind me of her state of undress and how easily the cold reaches her bones. I stand beside the walker and wait for her shaking body to maneuver into the seat before wheeling her into the bathroom.

It's a tedious process to strip her of the remaining items and position her in the shower. Even without the weight and height of the boot, she is too unsteady on her feet and relies far too heavily on both myself and the disabled aids meant to act as a prop rather than a crutch. Too much exertion from leaning on the shower chair could cause it to slip, resulting in her toppling over. Brittle bones losing the war against arthritis and osteoporosis would be the casualties in such a fall, not taking but a second to snap. Again. Despite the nonslip mat in the shower area, it's still a high radioactive zone when water is added.

"Brr. It's cold. Turn the water on, so the steam warms the room."

I do as she asked, not bothering to comment that I just turned it off. When she's ready, I hand her a soaped-up washcloth and the shower hose before waiting outside the closed glass partition. Condensation clings to the cold mirror as the humidity within the compact bathroom rises. I would turn the fan on or crack the window to clear the expanding mist, but I know she'd get upset and complain I was sucking all the heat from the room. It's not worth the argument, and I'm surprised with how well I'm becoming accustomed to second-guessing her.

My head lolls back briefly, and I wonder what I did to deserve to be here right now. Almost every minute of my day has become consumed by her. I should feel content, being here to help her through this rough time—to be the child she always wanted me to be—if only she wasn't so stuck in her ways and overly demanding.

It's not her fault. She's now incapable of doing most of the everyday tasks herself.

As if on cue, her softly spoken words break into my thoughts.

"I can't reach my back. Can you wash it, please?"

She needs me.

ALL FOR MOTHER

Water sloshes out onto the tiles when I open the door, and I immediately point the streaming nozzle away. Vertebrae knuckle down the center of her bent back, mottled, loose skin draping haphazardly. Getting old is not dignified, nor is it for the vain. It must be frustrating for someone who was once so lively and proud to be in such a vulnerable position.

"Sure. Hand me the washcloth."

She does, and I lightly rub it in small circles across her back, forcing myself into that clinical mindset. The doctor said to keep an eye out for any non-blanchable spots of redness that could be the start of a bedsore. He was mainly referring to her feet, but I read in an online forum that lying or sitting in the same spot with limited mobility can easily cause these sores to develop and turn into festering ulcers.

"That feels good." Her body straightens, and she rolls her shoulders as the hot water streams off her back, taking the soap bubbles with it.

I quickly avert my gaze, unsuccessfully trying to unsee the elongated breasts hanging down her stomach. My abrupt reaction accidentally jerks the shower nozzle, and water streams higher onto her thinning head.

"Ash! You're wetting my hair," she screeches. "Watch what you're doing."

In our slowed haste to get Mother into the shower, we forgot the shower cap.

"It's okay. It didn't get that wet. I can towel-dry it for you."

"Great." Her tone is biting, and she looks over her shoulder to flash her ire at me. "Fluffy, knotted hair isn't something I hoping to achieve today. Can't you do anything right?"

My eyes lift and then break contact with hers. I watch the building condensation form into droplets and trickle down the tiled walls. Slowly, slowly before building momentum and sliding to the floor. The movement is calming and gives me the chance to school my features and compose myself before responding.

"I'm sorry. It was an accident." I put an extra bite of cheer in my voice and hope it's contagious. "Don't forget, tomorrow's Friday, and Ms. Suzy will be able to fix it."

The reminder of her salon appointment appeases her slightly.

"Yes. Well then, I suppose it's fine. It's fine. Yes, it's fine." Her words are muttered more to herself than to me. I ignore them.

"Let's get you dried and into clean clothes, so you can catch your movie."

The arduous chore of toweling her off and getting her safely out of the shower is not without risk. Her hands death-grip my arm, fingers wrapped like a vise. Eyes crinkle and lips purse on a whimper as she puts weight on her broken leg. I drape her robe around her shoulders when she's out and seated again on the walker and gently pull her legs through a clean incontinence diaper. Her now-quivering arms rise enough for me to pull the nightgown on her before I wheel her back to the bedroom, so she can sit more comfortably on her bed while I inspect her foot.

There are no new abrasions or blisters.

"My skin's dry. Can you rub some lotion into it? I can't reach my feet, and I'm scared I'll fall if I try."

Mother runs hot and cold. I'm either being the most helpful person in the world or the most incompetent. Her words and attitude give me whiplash, and over the past days—even before she broke her leg—lines have blurred so much that half the time, I can't even remember which one I'm meant to be. She yells at me one minute, and the next, she asks me to rub cream on her body.

It takes all my energy to submit and allow myself to roam into an emotionless void of nothingness. I reach for the plastic bottle and pour the scented liquid into my hand.

ALL FOR MOTHER

With a deep breath, I massage it into her body, ignoring the satisfied whimpers.

"That feels so much better already. Thank you."

"You're welcome," is my hollow reply.

Fuck my life.

Eleven

It's Friday.

For most, this would be the time to get excited about the forthcoming weekend, plans for an evening out with friends, dinner dates. That's what normal people do—those who have a life. At the moment, I unfortunately don't. Today's the day Mother gets her hair done. Her standing appointment at the salon is at noon every Friday until eternity.

"Ash."

Ugh.

Mother has been calling out in the mornings for me to help her up to use the bathroom, but she's bellowing out earlier than usual. It's not a good sign if she's awake before seven a.m., as it can only mean a few things—and none of them good. She probably didn't sleep well. If that's the case, then the rest of the day is going to be miserable as she attempts to take out her inability to sleep drug-free on everyone around her. I tell her to take the painkillers. That's what they're for and why the doctor prescribed them.

"Ash!"

I reluctantly roll out of bed and pull on the discarded sweats from yesterday. Her being irritable is really nothing new. It hasn't been taking much to set her off to whine and complain. It could be the weather—it's too hot or too cold. Maybe it rained or didn't rain enough. Her heel rubbed on her shoe, and the over-the-top thread count sheets are nothing better than sandpaper rubbing her skin raw.

Finger-combing my hair, studying the disheveled reflection in the bathroom mirror, I decide I need more sleep. And a break. Having her call out now, on a Friday—her day to be beautified and to have lunch at a café of her choosing within the community—does not bode well for either.

I carefully enter the darkened room, not wanting to make any sudden movements to scare her. She frightens easily, which is a mystery to me since the house couldn't be more secure with locks engaged on every window and dead bolts on all doors. The black-out curtains sway slightly, allowing a sliver of sunlight through, and I silently berate myself for not ensuring the heavy material overlapped when they were drawn closed last night.

"Good morning, Mother." I decide not to turn on the lights or open the curtains. The natural light permeating through the opaque glass in the en suite bathroom provides muted light into the room once the sliding door is pushed open. "Did you sleep well?"

Fingers white-knuckle the duvet cover and hold it up to her chin, eyes looking over to me expectantly.

"I need to use the bathroom." Her labored breathing is interrupted by the barely audible words.

There's no *hello* or *good morning*, and my question as to whether she slept well is only answered with a grunt. She's lying on her back, unmoving other than blinking wide eyes with the introduced brightness. This is the position I left her in when I tucked her into bed last night. I gently pull back the duvet and sheet to the end of the bed, exposing her delicate legs, scarcely covered by the flannel nightdress. It's her favorite—short sleeves and covered in tiny blue flowers. The pungent stench of urine wafts up and spreads through the room.

ALL FOR MOTHER

Ever so slowly, she rolls to her side and slides her feet closer to the edge of the bed. Her movements are jerky, and she whimpers quietly, complaining about the pain in her knee. The action causes the hem to rise, and the yellowed padding of the adult diaper becomes visible. It's full.

With shaking arms, she attempts to push up into a sitting position. I stand to her flank and watch, not offering to help. This isn't a punishment or a test. I see it more as a way for her to try and engage her muscles. She has to make an effort. I can't let her get lazy or too reliant on me because her muscles will end up in a state of atrophy.

"Can you help me, please? I'm dizzy. So, so dizzy." Today looks to be no different, and she falls back down, crying. Tears—either real or crocodile—run down her cheeks. "I can't get up. I just can't."

Her feeble words and admission for help spring me into action. She tried. And failed. A lot of my reasons for how I've been responding to her are more selfish and maybe even duplicitous. I really want her to acknowledge me for me and what I'm doing to help, even when she thinks I'm not. There's a lot of denial on her behalf that I'm not useful, but she'll come to realize at some stage that it's not the case. I wish she'd appreciate me more and treat me less like a servant. To just see me, Ash. Her Ash.

I offer my hand. I enclose my fingers around her fragile wrist and pull her up, ensuring her feet swing down and around at the same time. I've already positioned the wheelie walker in front of her, brakes engaged, and wait to see if she has the energy to make it to the toilet under her own steam. If she doesn't, I'll help her sit on the chair and push her into position.

"Thank you," she says.

Although she's faint—or claims to be—she decides to try and make it herself. Weak arms shake as she somehow manages to get upright, disengages the brakes and shuffles in the direction of the bathroom.

"Stay close in case I get dizzy again."

I acquiesce because it's easier that way, and I slowly follow along behind her. The nine-foot journey to the toilet is as much tedious as it is perilous. After she backs up to the commode, I make sure to engage the braking mechanism on the walker, as it's one thing she occasionally forgets to do, and move to the side in readiness.

I watch on in silence, waiting for the next prompt—be it physical or verbal—to work out what she expects from me. How I can help. We've been here before, and I keep quiet, tasting the air, trying to determine the balance of her spirit. Unfortunately, all my palate picks up is the cloying waft of ammonia, which seems to have followed us into the bathroom.

Depending on her strength and mood, she'll either ready herself to sit or flounder and wait for me to do it. Today seems to be a good day, her balance and arms deciding to act in sync. Once freed from its hold on her hips, the diaper slips to the tiled floor and lands with a thud. I ignore it, watching to ensure the skirt of her dress is clear of the seat before she tries to lower herself.

"You okay?" I can't help but ask, compassion lacing my tone.

"Mmhmm," she grunts her response before the aluminum white legs of the toilet aid creaks in distress, assaulted with her weight from above. *Thud-pfft.* The motion expels unwanted gas from the internal confines of her body.

I take leave and offer her the freedom to pee in solitude, although there is no privacy. As much as I wish it to be, it's just an illusion. My head rests on the doorjamb, and I close my eyes to monitor the tinkle of fluid as it lands in the bowl. She huffs and shuffles a bit as more unwanted gas and fluid are discharged. The scuffling of her feet during this process pushes the filled diaper around on the tiles, marking her territory, not unlike a dog marking theirs.

Rushing water sounds after she initiates the flush and flags my next task. I reenter the room, ensuring to grab a new diaper from the cabinet as I do. She sits with her arms on the rails, attempting to push up.

"Do you want to wash up a bit and put on a clean diaper?" Anticipating her answer, I prepare a warm washcloth.

"Yes, I suppose I should." She shifts uncomfortably.

I gingerly pick up the soiled pants between two fingers and toss it in the white trash can. The lavender-infused bin lining should mask the odor, but it doesn't. The lid has a great seal, so as long as it's closed, it allows us to blissfully ignore the contents.

"Best to clean up as much as I can before we head out to the salon. I'm sure Suzy won't appreciate me smelling like a bar's urinal at happy hour."

I chuckle at her attempted humor and its visual. Her hairdresser is an angel in disguise. She has the patience of a saint and a heart of gold. Clichés to be sure but true nonetheless. I'm fairly confident, however, that any lingering smell of urine wouldn't be noticed over the hairspray fragrance at Suzy's salon.

"Here you go." I hand her the washcloth and remove the dirty nightgown, pulling it over her head. It's damp around the hem, and I wash my hands after tossing it in the laundry basket.

"You might need to do my back." She holds out the cloth with a trembling hand before averting her eyes to the floor.

Her weakened voice wrenches my heart and reminds me why I'm here. I gently sponge her clean and wheel her back to the bedroom to help her dress for today's outing.

Every day has its challenges, and everyday, ordinary activities I take for granted are becoming more and more difficult for her. I wish she'd realize how taxing it is for me to keep up with the facade of everything being normal. It's so easy for her to be chauffeured to her appointments, helped every step of the way. To sit and wait while I prepare or order her meals. To check her in for her appointments and fill out any necessary paperwork. I've been so cooperative and compliant for all of this. There are some weekly rituals I wish she'd surrender, but she refuses to let them go even though they end up consuming so much of my time. It's also doubly frustrating when she decides to make decisions and demands on the fly, throwing out all of my attempts at scheduling and organization.

We're seated in a booth at her and Father's favorite Italian bistro. The after-lunch crowd is sparce, not filling the space as it does during the peak meal times. The customers during the day are mainly moms with babies or toddlers. I'm flustered, perspiration trickling down my back as I try to regain my breath after the hassle of swapping out the wheelchair for the walker at the last minute and assisting her into the small restaurant. Prior to arriving here, we stopped at the pharmacy and Hallmark store for no other reason than picking up some cards and candy. I'd hoped our outing for her hair appointment and lunch would be done and she'd be resting in her chair, taking an afternoon nap. The additional stops and her need to utilize the facilities have stressed me out and screwed with my afternoon plans to meet up with Joel during his break.

She hadn't asked. She'd just expected me to follow through with her request. More fool me because I did, texting Joel to cancel.

"Mrs. Doyle. How lovely to see you." The owner, Mr. Russo, hovers by my chair, facing Mother. "I was sorry to hear about Robert. How have you been?"

ALL FOR MOTHER

His bright smile turns somber, and he reaches over to gently pat Mother on her arm.

"Thank you. Missing Bobby, obviously, but he's in a better place now." Her head bows solemnly, eyes glistening, providing the expected and respectful answer. After a beat, she sits up, pulling her shoulders back, and clutches her hands together on the table. "I've been better though. Did you notice my latest accessory?" One hand gestures toward the cumbersome black plastic swallowing half of her leg.

"I did," he says with a laugh, following the direction of her hand. "What did you do to yourself?"

She leans forward and whispers in a conspiratorial tone, "I fell in my kitchen and broke my tibia in two places. This moon boot is rather annoying, but I'm managing fine."

Lies. Her words are lies. She's not *managing fine*.

Mr. Russo nods and chuckles as though everything she said makes perfect sense. Turning to me with a tight smile, he says, "You must be Ash. I'm so glad you're here, helping your mama through this difficult time."

My face is frozen, cheeks aching and lips stretched in what I hope is seen as congenial and not a grimace. "I'm trying, sir."

He tips his head, wishes us a pleasant meal, and excuses himself to return to the kitchen. Mother immediately starts prattling on about how wonderful he is and how great the food and service are here. We place our order with the young waitress, and then Mother continues her babbling. Her hair salon, I've come to believe, is more a meeting place for women to go and gossip. Tall tales told of husbands, neighbors, and church friends. A little network of scandalmongers, congregating around the wash basin to off-load their weekly news. I'm sure after our lunch today—as with every Friday lunch—there'll be nothing I won't know about Suzy and her family, extended relatives included, as well as the myriad of other faceless names they gossip about.

It's a welcome break to the one-sided natter when the food is placed in front of us. Mother ordered the minestrone soup with a salad while I would never say no to a bowl of ravioli. All the excitement of the day and the early morning start is wearing on her. She's tired but trying to remain graceful in case anyone is watching.

"How's your soup?"

"It's great. The best in the state for sure." Her shaking hand manages to spoon liquid into her mouth with minimal spillage. She reaches across the table to snag a piece of the warm bread, and the cuff of her shirt drags in her bowl, tinged red liquid seeping slightly in the weave up the sleeve.

"What are you doing?" she asks, trying to snatch away the arm I've caught, holding it up as I move the soup out of the way and use my napkin to dab at the wetness. She quiets when she realizes what she's done. Face flushed, she whispers, "Thank you."

"It's not a problem. I almost did the same," I say, lifting my arms above the almost-empty plate of ravioli, trying to take away some of her embarrassment.

She smiles and goes back to her food, spooning and chewing softly in silence. I see it before it happens; she rolls up her sleeve slightly and reaches across the table again for another piece of bread. Just like the last time, her sleeve drags through the soup. I sigh as I move her bowl again and wipe up the mess as best as I can before taking a quick look around the restaurant. Most of the other moms are looking in our direction and smiling. They probably think it's a nice thing to see, a role reversal of their current situation with the child now caring for the mother. That there's love between us, bonding us together. But it's an act. A charade. A simple to and fro of nothing more than necessity. I'm not really here out of loyalty or some bond-like thing that they currently have with their newborn baby or toddler.

I'm starting to wonder why I am actually here.

With new eyes, I again look around the restaurant and realize there's not much difference between me and these mothers. By watching, I determine that they have it somewhat easier than me. Unlike my mother, their children learn from their mistakes.

Having suddenly lost my appetite, I place my flatware down and sit back. "I'm ready to go when you are, Mother."

TWELVE

I enter her room and pull the curtains back.

"I want to know why I'm so dizzy."

Not again.

"It will pass. Just give it a minute."

She's complained of this in one way or another every day since the accident. I've spoken to her doctor, and there's no medical reason for this. Joel said it's probably from staying motionless in one position for too long, like when she sleeps. Of course, Mother wants all the tests run in case she's dying of some rare dizziness-induced disease, but both Joel and her doctor agree it would be a waste of time. None of the explained logic helps stop the constant grumbling.

"You don't know that."

"No, but I'm sure it'll pass."

I tune her response out, converting it to white noise. It helps me focus on everything and nothing at the same time and provides me with the strength to carry out the tasks she expects from me. Making it impersonal allows my mind to wander, disassociating the mundane of our routine and imagining my day anywhere but here. It's how I've been coping. In her eyes, I'm the epitome of a compliant child. Helping. Listening. Following instructions. So caught up in her own insular world, she fails to realize my responses are nothing more than well-timed grunts aimed at keeping the peace and getting us both through the never-ending hours. The days have turned into short sound bites played constantly on repetition.

"Here, Mother." I place my hand under her arm to help her stand.

"Ow!" Her cry freezes me in place. "You're hurting me. Why would you do that?" Malice threads through her declaration, and I let go of her, speechless.

She's standing, albeit unsteadily, with one hand death-gripping the walker and the other rubbing the area where I was holding her.

"I'll probably need surgery on this shoulder now. You're doing this on purpose. Why?"

Words fail me. I can't think of a single thing to say. My hands tremble, and I quickly move them behind my back as though they were a guilty coconspirator in something I'm not aware of.

"N-no, Mother. I-I didn't do anything—mean to do anything," I say, ears ringing and blinking back tears. "I-I'm sorry. I thought I was being gentle. If I hurt you, it was an accident. I was only trying to help."

"Be careful then. And stop stuttering like a child." She clears her throat and stares at the wall.

All of her energy and weight is directed to the walker, propelling her forward in the direction of the bathroom. Walking. The wheels emit a slow squeal with the force of every labored revolution.

In zombie-like fashion, I shuffle my feet behind hers, hands twitching, ready to step in if her legs give out or her hands let go of the frame. A safety net, trailing behind. Doing my duty. But for what?

Her outburst has me both confused and perturbed for the first time since I've been here, caring for her. I've dealt with her forgetfulness and mostly unintended impoliteness almost daily. General annoyance is something I've become used to feeling. Being unsettled is new, especially when I was hoping she was finding me helpful. Obliging.

ALL FOR MOTHER

Considerate. Maybe even grateful for everything I was doing to help. But to accuse me of purposely hurting her physically ...

I stand clear as she maneuvers around to back up to the privy, allowing the soiled diaper to drop to the tiled floor with its muted thwack. The plastic toilet aid towers over the white porcelain, and she falls, ungracefully sitting with a violent thud. Acting the dutiful child, I bend to retrieve the heavy urine-filled pants and dispose of them before retreating to the bedroom.

She strains over the toilet, and I busy myself, checking the bed for damp spots from any leakages. Finding it wet, I rip the sheets off to replace them with the clean set I washed yesterday and lament the fact that I'll have to do another load today. The grunting and strained whimpers from the other room finally turn to a sigh of relief as her bowels empty. My eyes close briefly as I desperately want to ignore the sounds, but I know it'll be easier for me to preempt her wants by unfortunately tuning in.

But is that the problem—me wanting to anticipate her every need? Wanting to please her? And for what—for her to turn around and accuse me of something I didn't do? I look down at my hands again, wondering if I did in fact grip her too tightly.

I numbly continue to straighten up the room, foreseeing what comes next. As expected, her defecation's a short-lived victory, and I envision the different muscles now struggling with the task of unraveling the toilet tissue needed to wipe away the mess. The gurgles and groans let me know she's not done. Not yet anyway.

A final sob with the finale being the flush is my signal she's done, and I return into the room as she struggles to push up from sitting. I don't rush to help her like I would any other time. Instead, I keep my distance and wait for her to ask for my help. Her eyes look at me questioningly.

Has she already forgotten the way she snapped at me ten minutes ago? Can she not understand my hesitation now?

"Hang on," I speak softly, pasting on a forced smile. "Do you want to put on a fresh diaper?"

She sinks back down, shoulders hunched, rubbing the end of the floral nightgown between her fingers. My nose wrinkles at the distinct smell of urine mixed with old age as I crouch before her.

"Lift," I say, tapping one leg, putting the bare foot through the leg hole before following the same procedure with the other. "Lift."

"You're doing it again," she says, kicking her leg out toward me.

"I'm doing what?" I stand and look down at her, our eyes meeting.

Her reddened face highlights flattened lips in a wavering sneer.

"What do you think I'm doing? What's going on?"

Her body trembles. "You were hitting me," she says, voiced raised and filled with spite.

Our eyes collide as I digest her accusation before I turn and abruptly leave the room.

What the hell?
Where has this come from?

I've been here now for months, looking after her. Caring for her. Being her chauffeur, running her errands, cleaning, cooking. Everything. I've sat by and listened as she tells her stories of the past and gossips about neighbors and people at church. I've lost sleep while I've been at her beck and call, doing everything I can think of to make all of this as comfortable as possible. For both of us but mainly for her.

The blinds in my room are open, and the morning sun streams in, providing limited warmth, as I pace between the bed and my suitcase. My hands shake, fists opening and closing of their own accord, not knowing if they should be picking up my belongings and packing them away. I flop on the bed and reach over to unplug my phone from its charging port. I can't stay here anymore;

my sister will have to step in and come up with an alternative solution for the remaining few weeks Mother has the boot on.

My fingers are poised over Bel's name, but I can't bring myself to press the Call button. I want to, but I can't. With a groan, I drop the phone beside my head and cover my face with my hands. If I admit failure, then everything everyone has ever said about me will be validated in their unseeing eyes. Although I'm certain the relatives are relieved; they're not the ones responsible for caring for Mother. They're probably taking a vested interest in whether I will stay the course. I don't want to, but I think I'm committed until she gets the wretched boot off.

Maybe I've been overly complacent with everything. The doctor and even Joel have spoken to me about the deterioration of the mind in the elderly. Paranoia. Hallucinations. Apathy and withdrawal. Confusion. Rapid mood swings. Personality change. All things that can point to the onset of dementia. I'm positive Mother can tick a few of those off the list this morning.

She wants me here; I'm sure of it. I can't let her mind play tricks and force me away with words and actions she doesn't really mean. She needs me, and I'm committed to see this through.

With a sigh, I roll over onto my stomach and send a short text message off to Joel. He always has the best advice or words of encouragement, and right now, I could do with both.

But first, Mother ... I left her sitting, half-dressed, on the toilet.

When I reenter the bathroom, I see she's managed to pull up the incontinence pants, and she is trying to stand. Sagging skin draped over frail bones quiver as she makes it halfway. I quickly interject, gripping an arm, being careful to monitor the pressure so as not to hurt her or leave a bruise.

"I'm not dressing today," she whispers, not making eye contact. "But I'll need a clean nightdress. I-I'm not sure if I dirtied this one. I can't tell if it's wet. But I think it smells."

There's no apology, not that I expected one. In my absence, she was obviously struggling to leave the bathroom, and I can tell from her current demeanor that the task was beyond her. I want to gloat, to rub in the fact that I'm not here to bully or harm her but to care for her. She's hopefully realized that some of the simplest of tasks are currently out of her reach and she needs my assistance.

I plaster a fake smile in place. "Of course, Mother. We can do that."

Thirteen

Another day means another longer night. My life is morphing into one big, complicated, never-ending cycle. Hopefully, Mother will have a pleasant evening, go to bed early, and allow me to sneak out for a few hours.

"Are you ready for dinner?" I ask, walking into the room, food already prepared and on a tray.

It's been easier, bringing everything to her. I should be making her walk to the kitchen and sit at the table, but it's an effort, getting her in there. The dining chairs are uncomfortable and don't offer any support. They're also too low for her to sit, safely unassisted, and I've been trying to keep my manhandling of her to a minimum.

She's watching the news, legs up, seat reclined. Her eyes sparkle, and if she wasn't so prim and proper, I'm sure she'd be rubbing her hands together in glee, indicating my timing tonight is perfect.

If I'd been earlier, she'd have waved me off and ignored the food on the tray. By the time she got around to the food, it would've cooled, any oil on the plate hardening into an off-colored, gel-like substance. She'd have picked at it and pushed bits around the plate before placing the napkin and some used tissues on top, asking for her ice cream dessert.

"Smells divine," she says, lowering her chair and pulling the hospital-styled over-bed table in front of her. "What is it?"

"Chicken." I carefully place the tray down, making sure the water doesn't spill.

The crusted Southern-styled legs are golden brown and sit next to a pile of rice covered with Mediterranean-spiced pan-grilled vegetables. I know she's not a fan of red onion or peppers, but the presentation of her plate rivals some of the nicer restaurants in the area—those who use preprepared or frozen packet meals anyway.

She picks up the egg cup to the side of her water, containing her nightly medication, and shakes it gently. "What are the extra white ones? Why are they there? And where's the Tylenol?"

She's fastidious about her medication, and there's a bunch of pills she takes both morning and night. I've been able to work out what they're for based on conversations between her and the doctor and my own Google research. It's probably best that I've taken over in dispensing them.

One's for her heart; it's the one I have to cut into quarters, using a pill splitter. There's a low-dose aspirin, which has to do with the heart as well. Something for blood pressure—an anti-inflammatory. And then there's the pill she's been taking for the past few days for her upset stomach—an aftereffect from some of the pills. On the box, it says it's for reflux and stomach acid, and a side effect for this one is constipation, which warrants the two colored stool-softener pills. I think if she were to read the actual details for all of these meds, she wouldn't be taking half the pills her doctors have told her to take.

"The smaller one is the Valium," I remind her. She's been taking that one lately to help her sleep at night. "And the other is codeine, for the pain."

Her cheeks suck in while she purses her lips. "I don't want the painkillers. I want Tylenol."

ALL FOR MOTHER

I knew this argument was coming. She's been whining all day about the throbbing in her leg and foot. Partly from the blisters that have formed on her heels and toes and the other from the compression and weight of the boot. I'm also sure whatever goes on with the actual healing of the bones is contributing as well.

"The doctor said you can take both if you need to. You've been in so much pain today. I thought this would help and allow you to get some sleep."

"I don't want it."

Spittle flies from her mouth, and she thrusts the pill cup toward me. With a sigh, I flick through the pills and remove the offending one.

"That's okay," I say, placing it back down next to her water. "I brought it out in case you wanted it; that's all."

"Once you start taking those, you can't stop. The doctor also said they'll block me up."

I shake my head and try not to chuckle. Of all the pills I've doled out tonight, it's only the stool softener that doesn't have the side effect of constipation listed on the box. And that's the one she normally won't take because it won't guarantee the exact moment she'll have a bowel movement. A crappy predicament to be in for sure.

"That's what the Senna's for. But it's okay. I'll put it back."

I'm halfway out of the room when she replies, "Make sure you do."

I turn around and stare at her, mouth agape. "I'm sorry, what?"

Surely, she doesn't mean what I think she means.

"I said, make sure you put it back. Don't want you getting any ideas about popping my pills." She picks up her fork in one hand and starts trying to break off parts of the chicken with its tines.

The thought has crossed my mind on multiple occasions. I've spent time glaring at the bottles of codeine and Valium, wondering what it would be like to just not feel or care for an afternoon.

"That's how kids become junkies. I've seen the news." Her head bobs with the seriousness of her observation.

A small, incredulous laugh escapes, and not wanting to get into an argument about her ill-informed opinions, I leave the room to replace the codeine with acetaminophen.

Although I have no desire to start a disagreement, I want her to take the codeine. I don't like the fact that she's in pain and she refuses to take what was prescribed by her doctor to counter it. It confounds me why she won't take them, pooping excuses aside. I have this theory about it being related to her perceived prestige and being able to tell her friends that she didn't succumb to any of the drugs or needing them post-healing. It's the most ridiculous reason, but somehow, it makes sense.

Old people can be so obstinate, and in long doses, it's frustrating.

I do need her to sleep well tonight—at least initially—so I can escape for a bit to relax and catch my breath. There's a sports bar on the edge of the neighborhood, frequented by those living in the area. Joel recommended it, and I was hoping to enjoy a few stolen moments to meet up with him. The painkiller would have worked in well with the Valium and helped her drift off into an uninhibited sleep.

What if ...
It won't hurt ...
It couldn't hurt ...

Our deal was for me to be here to help her, not to be her day caregiver and night nurse. Although I understand she's in pain and her mobility's affected, I don't see why I have to be here twenty-four/seven, except for when she thinks I'm running errands for her.

I grab the mortar and pestle to grind one of the codeine pills down, the pestle finding initial resistance from the tablet. It takes a bit of additional pressure, like there's an armored coating on the outside, but once through, it crumbles into fine particles. I lick my finger to capture a few of the fine specks to gauge the taste. It has a very strong and distinctive flavor, and I worry that it'll be noticeable, sprinkled over her food.

Perspiration beads on my top lip as I look around the kitchen to identify something I know she'll eat without question. Chocolate ice cream topping. She's a sucker for anything with chocolate. I can definitely add it to the syrup and present her with the dessert treat after her dinner. Without overthinking it, I pour some into a mug and grind down a second pill before adding the white powder. Stirring the two together, I notice the white powder isn't absorbing into the chocolate. The normal silken, smooth texture is marred and has more of a grainy one.

"Shit. Shit. Shit," I mutter to myself while continuing to stir, hoping it becomes less visible.

"Ash, where's the Tylenol?" her voice calls from the other room.

"Great." I push the mug and spoon back along the counter with an air of disgust. Staring at it, I will a solution to come to me. I don't want to miss out on my date with Joel tonight.

Date?

It's not a date. He's just being polite and trying to help me out during this confusing period of uncertainty. There could be a spark, but we're too different, and we never would have met if it wasn't for the moon boot. But is it kismet?

"Ash! Tylenol!"

"Shit." I swipe my forehead and let my hands fall to the counter, watching my knuckles whiten as they clench into fists. "Fucking Lifetime movies."

Does kismet make you drug your dependent mother?

"Screw it."

I grab the ice cream and scoop a serving into a bowl. Then, I generously pour all of the tainted syrup from the mug on top. Grabbing everything else I need, I return to Mother.

"Here you go. I brought the Tylenol, and I also brought some ice cream."

The ice cream acts as bait for her good behavior, and I'm rewarded with a rare smile of gratitude. My insides twist, and I gulp down the guilt as her eyes light up at her treat. In this moment, she doesn't realize that I have taken away one of her basic rights. I'm going to drug her, so I can go out. My hands shake, and I hesitate, taking a small step backward with half a thought to dispose of it down the sink when her greedy little hands reach out and take it from me.

"Thanks, Ash."

She fills the spoon and shoves it in her mouth, attention now back to the television. I struggle with opening the bottle of Tylenol, not taking my eyes off her as she swallows spoonful after spoonful of the dessert.

"Here."

She removes two tablets from my open palm and gulps them down with the rest of her water.

"That was great. You outdid yourself tonight."

"Thank you, Mother," I say softly, pulling the table away from her and loading everything onto a tray to take back to the kitchen. "I'll clean these and be back to help you to bed."

"Mmhmm." She dismisses me with a nod, and the hydraulics of the chair are engaged as she settles back to continue watching her show.

The tray collides with the countertop on an angle, causing a loud ruckus. I ignore it as my hands cover my mouth and rock back and forth from my heels to my toes. My eyes search the ceiling for answers and forgiveness as my body quakes with the knowledge that I just drugged my mother.

A quick Google search informs me that crushing the two painkillers won't do anything to hurt her other than

ALL FOR MOTHER

help her have a rested sleep—just as the doctor prescribed. He certainly didn't prescribe underhanded tactics in getting her to take them though. The only thing that concerns me is the acetaminophen she unknowingly took as a drug chaser. But it should be fine. We will see.

I settle my nerves enough to tidy up and fill the time needed until I can put her to bed.

Before I realize it, my sketchbook's in hand, and I've used charcoal to explore the page with thick and thin lines, depicting a nightmarish scene. It's abstract, but through its strokes, all I can see is confusion and death.

"Way to go, Ash. Way to make yourself feel better ..." I mumble, tearing out the page and balling it up before tossing it toward the wastebasket in the corner of my room.

I enter the sunroom not long after and notice Mother's slackened features as she lies, reclined in her chair. She slowly blinks once and smiles when she realizes I'm there.

"Dinner was so good. Did I thank you for it?"

"Yes, Mother, you did."

"Good," she says, raising the chair as I position her walker in front of her. "I'd hate to have forgotten my manners."

I nod. It seems to be a better response than shrugging, and I'd hate to try and vocalize my thoughts on when she does or says things because it's an expected nicety rather than sincere.

Her movements are slow, and it seems to take us twice as long to walk to her bedroom and then through to the bathroom. I help her sit, and then I go and pull down the sheets for her. Once she's done, I guide her onto her bed and squat down in front to remove the shoe and sock of the unbooted foot.

"Ow!" She winces as I drag the sock down, giving it a good yank at the bottom to get it over the heel and off.

My eyes close as I wonder not for the first time if some of her reactions aren't feigned. It's been over an hour since I dosed her up with painkillers, and by her earlier relaxed state, I thought that they'd kicked in. It certainly appeared so. But now, she's tsk-tsking me for an action that shouldn't have hurt her at all.

"You need to be gentler. I don't want to have to wear two of these things," she says, kicking out the leg bound in black plastic.

It was accidental, and my eyes plead with hers to understand.

Not bothering to respond, I stand and lift her legs into the bed, swinging them around and helping her straighten them out. Her nightgown has risen slightly, and I tug the hem to cover her thighs. She lies there, watching, sucking in on her bottom lip. These actions with her little whimpers previously led me to believe she was in pain. Wounding her lip in an effort to redirect the pain from her knees to the area she's biting. It always made me feel a bit bad, having inflicted even the smallest level of pain.

Aging is the cruelest of jokes, slowly stripping away everything you've strived to build quickly and doing so without consideration. Seeing such a rapid decline over the past weeks—a reality that can't be faked—has me questioning all of my choices. We'll all end up here. At this same point. Unable to carry out the most basic of functions with arthritic hands, lacking the strength and mobility to open the bottle of medication, and flaccid arms, unable to pull open the fridge because of the weighted doors.

One day soon, there'll even be an inability to control body fluids. When that stage comes, she'll be happily housed in a new clinical-like abode. An assisted living facility providing the level of care required for the deteriorating mental and physical state. Once my father's life insurance is paid out, she can start looking at earnest into the type of establishment with the desired amenities for her.

But until then, she's stuck here and, for the time being, with me. Someone who was willing to spike her food with drugs to make her sleep.

Pulling the covers up to her neck, I sigh, feeling depressed due to the myriad of emotions that are playing havoc with my thoughts tonight. She misinterprets my ministrations for melancholy and somehow frees an arm from under the blankets, lifting it out toward me.

"Ash, say a prayer with me," she says before screwing her eyes closed so tightly that I can hardly see them among the sagging skin of the bunched-up wrinkles.

I place my hand in hers.

"Thank you, Lord, for today. Thank you for my Ash, for doing all the chores that I can't do and for looking out for me. Thank you for our health, and may my wounds continue to heal. Bless my family. We are your servants. Amen."

Her fingers squeeze mine with the final utterance, prompting me to say, "Amen," after sending my own silent prayer, asking for her not to overdose on the drugs I gave her and that she gets some pain-free rest.

I gently tuck her arm back under the covers, adjust the walker so she can reach it if she needs to, and turn the light off.

"Ash," she says before I exit the room, "I appreciate you."

"Thank you, Mother. Sleep well."

I turn back to take one last look at her before closing the door.

"Hey." Joel stands and steps out from the raised booth on the far wall of the sports bar and embraces me. It's comfortable and short-lived as he pulls away and returns to his seat.

My cheeks pinch with the forced smile I plaster on at his greeting, not able to shake my mood from earlier. "You look good out of scrubs," I say, pulling my phone out of my jacket pocket before taking it and my beanie off and sliding into the seat across from him.

This is the first time I've seen him out of his work attire, and he looks so relaxed, kicking back in his jeans and button-down shirt, whereas I feel dirty and on edge. My fingers nervously tap the table while I chew the inside of my cheek, looking around the room. It's not overly full, people mainly milling around the bar or watching the sports playing on the various TV screens at the industrial bar-height tables in front of them.

"You okay?" His eyes study me with concern. "You seem to be a bit quieter tonight. Nervous maybe?"

I offer him a tight-lipped smile and allay my still-tapping fingers, placing them in my lap. "I'm sorry. My mind's somewhere else at the moment."

"Your mother?" he asks. "How is she?"

There's a glass filled with water sitting off to the side that must have been poured for me. I reach across and take a big gulp.

"Sh-she's okay. Sleeping now. She took a few codeine before bed, so hopefully, she'll get the rest she needs."

He nods, and I can tell from his brown eyes that he believes my half-truth. Not that he'd have a reason to question it. It's normal for injured people or people with broken bones to take painkillers. For the pain. That's why they're prescribed. What I'm sure is not normal is for their children to grind them down and sprinkle them on top of their ice cream. I break eye contact, looking down at the menu before he can see the guilt.

"Is the break mending? You're coming up to the three-month mark now. You haven't been in for a review, or did you manage to sneak in on one of my days off?"

ALL FOR MOTHER

Three months.

How can it be three months already? It feels more like it's been three days, spanning over three years. Every day much like the one before. Groundhog Day.

The only reprieve I've been able to get from the monotony are the escapes to meet up with Joel, like this.

"Thanks for the reminder." I shake my head slowly and take a deep breath. "All of the days run together, and I've been losing time. I think we have the appointment scheduled for this coming week." My bottom lip trembles, and I lean forward onto my elbows and cover my face with my hands, attempting to keep the tears at bay.

"Shit," Joel whispers.

The scent of lemon and musk envelops me as strong arms wrap around my hunched shoulders, comforting me while silent sobs vibrate through my body. His warmth eases my heavy heart, a side effect from the past three months and possibly longer.

"I don't know if I can do this. I don't know … it's so hard," I say through ragged breaths.

"Shh. Of course you can. Everything will be okay. Your mom will be okay," Joel says softly into my hair.

I want to tell him that I'm not concerned with my mother right now, that my lapse in composure and my mini breakdown is more about me not wanting to be the one caring for Mother. That I'd rather be anywhere else, doing anything else. His sympathy and read on the situation are so very wrong.

"Your mother is so lucky to have you," he says.

I remember the satisfying popping sound as I crushed the pill before drugging her and purse my lips.

Nope, I don't think she is.

FOURTEEN

I've got a skip in my step this morning. I know I do. It's as though the wheelchair has grown wings and we're floating above the cracked pavement. We're off to the scheduled appointment to see if the bone has mended on her break. The last few weeks have been so painful ... for me. I've long since stopped caring about her pain levels.

But none of that matters today because today is the day she gets the boot off and I get my life back. Even her continuous talking on the drive over couldn't put a damper on what today means to me. I think I even laughed along with some of her stories. It was almost pleasant. Almost. My mind is clearer, and my heart feels lighter.

Automatic doors open as we approach and move from dull obscurity into the sparkling androgyny. My nose twitches at the antiseptic-filled air, and I cast my gaze around the room, searching. He's not at the desk, and I feel my feet faltering. The bubble of excitement felt moments before deflates somewhat, and I force the wheelchair to a standstill as I gather myself.

I hoped Joel would be out here at reception, but he's not. The woman sitting where I expected him to be looks up and offers a curt nod, acknowledging our arrival.

She pushes the blue frames up her nose before gesturing to the earpiece. "I'll just be a minute," she whispers. "Take a seat."

I wheel Mother to the end of the row of chairs, not bothering to engage the brakes, and reluctantly sit. The sterile state of the waiting room reminds me of the house, everything neat and in order. Overly bright lights show the absence of dust or debris, confirming regular cleaning. Waiting areas are so bland and boring. And quiet. It's like there's an unwritten rule for silence and good behavior. I refuse to let the uninspired surroundings lessen my mood.

I'm motioned over to the receptionist. The name tag on her blouse identifies her as Sandy, and she looks up at me expectantly.

"Mrs. Doyle," I say, indicating toward Mother. "She's got an appointment with Dr. Fredericks. A follow-up for her broken leg."

Sandy goes to type something into the computer when a flashing red light blinking on the phone console catches her attention. She sends an apologetic smile and mouths the word, *Sorry*, before checking something on the screen in front of her and clicking a button on her headset.

"Apollo Clinic. Is this an emergency, or can you hold for a minute, please?"

I wonder briefly why someone would call a doctor's clinic if it was an emergency and not 911.

"Sorry about that," Sandy says, looking up from the computer over her glasses. "Mrs. Doyle? Yes, I have her here. Are you the paid caretaker or a relative?"

"She's my mother. I've been taking care of her."

"Aw, how lovely for you two, spending this time together," she says overly brightly, clutching the chained cross hanging around her neck. "I hope my children are as thoughtful and caring as you if I ever get to that stage of needing help like this."

My cheeks freeze, pulling my lips into a false smile. She's not the first stranger to make a comment like this, approving of our family's seemingly happily ever after.

Initially, after Mother's fall, I was riddled with guilt and would get anxiety when I couldn't find the brands of items she'd specifically asked me to pick up for her. I'd question the shop assistants and watch their frustration or annoyance with my short temper due to lack of sleep. But as soon as I mentioned I was caring for Mother and how badly I needed to find these items for her, their demeanor would change dramatically. I went from a nagging, complaining, and maybe a little angry patron to this considerate and loving person they'd go out of their way to help. It was nice in the beginning and helped me navigate those early days, and I'd feed off the emotional support and praise from strangers. They made me feel special. When Mother claimed I was incompetent, I'd seek their words of reassurance, telling me how wonderful and useful I was.

It's uncomfortable now when people say things like that to me. I no longer seek the affirmations because it's all lies. I don't want the praise because I know this has been building to a nightmare rather than the sweet fairy tale these strangers want it to be. I'm just doing what I'm doing until the moment I can escape. And my exit strategy starts today.

Regardless of Sandy's words, I don't allow it to reduce the underlying excitement I have, being here for today's doctor's appointment.

"Yes, it's been lovely. We're very fortunate."

She doesn't seem to read my reaction correctly or note the sarcasm beneath my words. The keyboard clicks as deft fingers move across them. "When you head through, take a left and go to Radiology. They'll do the X-ray before you see the doctor. It'll take about twenty minutes for the imaging report to be ready, so I'll organize a consulting room for you to wait in once you're done."

I nod at her instructions and open my mouth to ask about Joel, but she's already talking into her headset again.

"Is everything okay, Ash?" Mother asks as I grip the handles and turn her around.

"Yes. Everything's fine. We need to get the X-rays first."

We wheel past reception, and Sandy smiles and waves to Mother as we pass. The hallway is well lit, and my heart skips a beat when I spy a pair of broad shoulders in scrubs ahead. But it's not him; the height and hair color are all wrong. Following Sandy's directions, we stop in front of the door marked *Radiology* and knock. It's answered straightaway by another scrubs-wearing employee who is not Joel. She makes quick work of ushering us in and setting Mother up on the bed before taking the digital images required of my mother's leg.

"So, how are you both today?" Dr. Fredericks greets us kindly.

"Good morning, Doctor," Mother says. "It's such a beautiful day out, don't you agree?"

Mother's been perky all morning, her good mood increasing with each person she talks to. If I wasn't so excited about what this appointment means for me, I'm sure I'd be sulking in the corner. Embarrassed by the way she treats people and the overshare of information.

"Yes, it is." The doctor sits in his chair, swiveling it to face the desk, and opens Mother's file.

"We're glad to be here," I say. "I'm not sure who hates that boot more—me or Mom. We'll both be happy to get rid of it."

Dr. Fredericks places the folder down and turns back toward us. "I'm sure it's made for some difficult times. Can we take the boot off, so I can look at the foot and leg, please?"

"Of course," I answer for her, knowing when he said *we*, he really meant me.

ALL FOR MOTHER

"How is your family, Doctor?" Mother sits back while I unfasten the Velcro straps, trying to start a conversation over my head.

"They're good, thank you. Can you take the sock off as well?"

I nod and peel the wool-blended garment over her ankle and off her toes.

"How many children do you have? Two, isn't it? How old are they now?"

I ignore Mother's banter and lift her leg, so the doctor can see her foot. "The boot's been rubbing in a few places, but I've been adding padding and taping them as best as I can. It seems to be working. Other than slight discomfort, there's no break of the skin or infection."

"Good job. That can sometimes be difficult. You've done well to keep the pressure sores at bay." His praise sends a warmth through me. He both appreciates and understands the lengths I've gone to, treating the pending blisters. "Two. I've a boy and a girl. Twins. And they're seven now."

"Twins. Oh my. Two little blessings sent from above. Twice the smiles, twice the love." I follow Mother's gaze and know what she's going to say next. "Your wife is so pretty. And she must be an angel in disguise with the patience of a saint to look after twins. I hope my Ash will have kids one day."

"Yes, my wife is special," he answers Mother. Then, he continues to give me directions, "You can put the sock back on now and the boot."

Boot? He wants the boot back on?

"What are you doing, Ash?" Mother pulls her leg back under the seat of the wheelchair, moving it away from the moon boot.

"The doctor asked me to put your sock and boot back on." The words are said slowly, my voice rising a few decibels with an increased emphasis on the enunciation of each syllable.

She's told me often that she finds it difficult to understand the lilt of the doctor's accent, which is absurd, as he's from upstate, not out of the country. Her hearing aids are in, but sometimes, she fakes deafness—maybe as a reminder to those around her that she's a woman of age, milking it for all the attention. Her hearing has been good all morning up until this point. Maybe it was the mention of the boot? I know it pricked up my ears.

"Everything seems to be fine with the care of your leg, Mrs. Doyle. Ash has been doing a wonderful job, taking care of you, by the looks of things. Let me check if the X-ray results are in and see what the status of the break is."

I fasten the final Velcro strap and see the confusion on Mother's face.

"He's going to look at the X-rays now," I say, wondering if she's following along.

"Oh, good. Good. The lady in Radiology was so nice, don't you think?" She nods and continues on with an alternate conversation, not quite on point.

I think it makes her feel more important to have an interpreter, as if I were working for her as hired help. What she doesn't realize is that I'd prefer to be the mouthpiece. She has no idea of what's being asked and how to answer anyway. She'd rather talk about the weather or the children displayed in the frame on his desk.

The doctor moves the mouse to the right of his keyboard and clicks it a few times, lips pursing as he studies something on the screen. His screen is at an angle, and I can't clearly see what he's looking at as he sits back in his chair, making small, discouraging clicking sounds. A loud, audible sigh accompanies him as he shuts the computer before he turns to us. There's a sharp knock on the door, and the same nice lady from Radiology, who Mother was talking about, enters and hands the doctor an oversize white envelope before exiting the way she came.

Bad news is written all over the doctor's face, and I brace myself for something I seriously don't want to hear.

ALL FOR MOTHER

He grunts once before pulling out the gray film and clipping them in place on the boxed light above the desk. The lit backdrop makes the images clear, and my ears fill with cotton as he gestures to parts of her foot. Bones. There are too many bones, but apparently, one of those bones is not fully healed.

"But she's done everything right. She's been off it, and she has worn the boot the entire time. Why hasn't it mended?" I can't believe this. It was meant to be straightforward.

The doctor chuckles softly at my tone and looks at me with the expression of one chiding a young child. "Your mother has osteoporosis, which means her bones are brittle. It's common in people of her age. Breaks can take longer to fuse back together. I think we're looking at six months for this one." His expression remains neutral, words matter-of-fact.

This was meant to be the day she got the boot off, the day she took responsibility for her own mobility and everything else that went with it. This was meant to be the day I won back my freedom.

"The only thing for you is to keep doing what you're doing. Manage the pain. Maybe look for a multivitamin with higher calcium or vitamin D levels to help speed along the process."

My throat closes up as I listen to his advice. *Manage the pain? What about my pain—the pain of dealing with this twenty-four/seven?*

"So, the boot stays on?" I ask, rehashing known information. It's folly to believe his answer will change, but maybe if phrased slightly differently, I'll get a more palatable response in return.

"Yes." Same answer.

"She's been having issues with how cumbersome it is, which is workable during the day when she's active and I'm there to help, but at night, it's creating some issues," I say, grasping at straws. Any straw, searching for a win.

"She's been complaining of an aching back from just lying in bed all night. In the same position. The weight," I emphasize, "she can't roll over or move it."

The doctor studies me before looking at my mother. "Any bed sores present on her back?" he asks, hand rising to rub his chin.

"I have scoliosis, and my back—"

"Not yet," I say over the top of Mother's words, jumping on the potential opportunity to make some changes. "But if she's just going to lie there in the same position for eight to ten hours, it'll only be a matter of time. Those pressure sores on her foot are painful enough for her."

His thoughtful eyes meet mine, and he hesitates before speaking, "I suppose there's no harm in her sleeping with the boot off then. We want to minimize any secondary issues and bed sores …"

His words trail off, and I think he's going to change his mind.

"She doesn't get up much during the night, and if she does, she calls out to me to help. We've been doing well with the incontinence pants as well. Not wearing the boot will help and allow her to get some quality rest," I speak quickly and don't check Mother's reactions to my words. I doubt she realizes what I'm negotiating, but she'll be upset if she hears me mention the adult diapers.

"She's not sleeping well?"

"It's been okay. Sometimes, she says the throbbing keeps her awake. Where the break is but also in her knees because the weight of the boot has it pulling the leg into an awkward position for most of the night."

He turns to his computer, and the printer whirs shortly after as it spits out paper. He signs both of the pages and hands them to me one at a time. "Trazodone, fifty milligrams. This is to be taken daily, at night after food, to help with the sleep. Lortab, thirty milligrams. It's a narcotic and for the pain. Take two but only when the pain

ALL FOR MOTHER

is unbearable and not with any Valium or codeine, as it can affect the respiratory system. You should have enough repeats for everything else."

More drugs. My head throbs as I try to remember everything the doctor just said. He stands, and I follow suit to take his outstretched hand.

"Good luck. Give the clinic a call if you have any questions." The handshake is firm and brief, and he turns to Mother and repeats the gesture. "Keep doing what you've been doing, and I'll see you in a few months, Mrs. Doyle. Good-bye."

I pocket the scripts and prepare Mother to leave. The bottom has fallen out of my world. I hoped that today was the day we could get rid of the life-sucker wrapped around her foot. I feel angry that her bones have not mended back together, but more so, I feel gutted. Completely and utterly gutted.

We stop at the desk before the exit for Mother to work out the insurance and co-payment for the consultation, and I lean back against the wall, letting the staff do all the work. My stomach clenches in a hardened mass, and I breathe slowly through the discomfort.

This morning, my stomach welcomed flitting butterflies of enthusiasm and eagerness in the dawn light. I allowed plans to form in my mind as the sun was popping up over the horizon, beckoning it to come and cast out the shadows that had fallen over me over the past three months. The deep-seated notion of neglect and hopelessness was starting to burrow into the sinewy part of my muscles, and I wanted—no, I *needed* for the sun's rays to burn them away.

I imagined a short getaway with Joel. Someplace warm with a beach and a bar. Fancy fruity drinks with their own little umbrellas. An idea started to form about a studio apartment with canvases and paint. Some thoughts of how I could meld traditional with abstract, paint and charcoal.

Dreams were starting to develop, including small cards and prints and an online store.

Stability.

Freedom.

Success.

The doctor's words have snuffed out that light.

Watching her babble away with strangers about things that don't concern her or them, I'm struck with a realization. I am expected to continue with her care.

It's not sustainable.

I close my eyes and swallow. The tightening of my chest makes it hard to breathe, and my hand moves to place splayed fingers over my heart.

I can't do it.

The lump of plastic on her leg is slowly but steadily sucking away my essence and turning me into a mindless, caregiving zombie. Surely, there must be money to pay for someone to do this or to put her into a facility with trained professionals. Can't people see I am not suited for this job? This unpaid and thankless job.

I won't do it.

FIFTEEN

"Bel, I can't do this anymore. You need to find someone or something else. I'm done. She's going fucking crazy, and so am I. I can't deal with it."

I flick open the shutters in my room, blinking rapidly as the bright light burns sunspots in my vision before snapping them closed. The outside world taunts me, reminding me that I'm stuck here, in this house. It's better if I don't look.

"We can't." My sister's voice comes from the phone sitting on the dresser across the room. "The insurance is held up in probate court for another few months. Dad didn't put the right information on his insurance forms, so it needs to be processed through probate in case someone else wants to make a claim for unpaid debt."

"Can they?" I ask.

"Can they what?"

I shake my head with frustration, not that she can see. "Make a claim. Who can make a claim? Or who would?"

None of what she's saying makes any sense. *Why would the state court hold Father's insurance payout captive? Who else would be entitled to it other than Mother?*

"I don't know. No one. But that's the law, and there's nothing I can do to speed it up." She sighs with frustration. "We're doing what we can to help cover the mortgage cost. The other death benefits that were paid out all went to cover outstanding bills they let slip when Dad got sick."

I nod in understanding, remembering the few letters Mother opened and the look of confusion, followed by devastation, on her face. That was shortly after the funeral, and we stopped opening any official-looking correspondence, deciding to send them directly to Bel—Father's executor—to handle.

"She has her pension, doesn't she? And his military pension—or part of it?"

"Yes, that's right. But if you leave, it won't cover Mother's costs, and we can't afford to pay for a caregiver or to put her into a care facility. We'd need to sell the house, and it's not a good time to do that. She'd lose too much money on the sale."

Why does everything have to be so hard? In the movies and on television, the lawyers just write checks and send them off to the beneficiaries. Why is death so inconvenient? I lie on the bed and watch the slow revolutions of the fan. Dust caked on the leading edge of the discolored blade reminds me of yet another incomplete chore on Mother's list. Another reason I don't want to stay.

"I-I can't…"

"If you can just wait until this insurance clears probate, I'll make sure you get reimbursed for your time. Please, Ash." Desperation laces Bel's plea. "I don't want her selling up if we don't have to."

I turn on my side to stare in the direction of the phone. *Cash reimbursement? Would the family be willing to allow me to continue on in something like a paid position?* It's tempting, but if there's no money to pay for a professional, there's no money to entice me to stay. To compensate for my suffering. I don't think it'll be worth my time.

"How much?" I ask more out of curiosity than anything else.

ALL FOR MOTHER

"Sorry, what?"

"How much will I be paid to care for Mother?" I say slowly. "I know you all think of me as this big failure, but I am the one here, doing the job that none of you have stepped up to do. You know Mother. You can imagine how frustrating this has all been for both of us. I have done things, seen things I cannot unsee."

Bel goes quiet over the phone. I continue on wondering if she is really serious and if I could actually get a fair reimbursement for my time.

"I realize you don't understand or appreciate who I am and what it is I do. But I can't continue to put my life on hold. I've turned down work to stay here. Work that I desperately wanted to take. You can understand that. You might not agree with my lifestyle choices, but I am suffocating here. And that work might not be there when you all decide I am no longer needed because someone else is willing to step in."

Silence fills the room, and I scoff, "Thought so."

"The payout is for one hundred and fifty thousand," she says quietly.

This is the first time she or anyone has talked actual numbers to me. It's not a lot of cash when you weigh up a lifetime of work and achievements. But it's substantial.

"The mortgage needs to be paid out—that's only fifty thousand. We thought we'd put the remainder of the money into a trust for any out-of-pocket costs. Looking long-term, any balance will probably go toward a deposit for buying into a full-service retirement facility. I'll talk to the lawyer and Mother when the time is right and see if we can pay you ten or maybe fifteen thousand dollars."

I sit up and tuck a stray lock of hair behind my ear, running through the numbers in my head. If they're going to dangle this carrot, then I am going to make sure I take what is reasonable. What I deserve.

"I want twenty."

"Ash—"

"No, don't. If I wasn't here and you kept the house, how much would it cost to have someone doing what I'm doing? Much more than that." I stand and start pacing, glaring toward the phone when she starts to answer. "Don't patronize me. I've been online. I know some of these places cost upwards of five thousand a month. Don't you think you're getting off lightly?"

"But you're living there. She's paying the bills."

"So what?" I come to a stop and cross my arms, sneering down at the phone. "I'm the one changing her incontinence pads and cleaning up the shit when she doesn't make it to the bathroom on time. And when I say *shit*, I mean, feces. I'm cooking for her, cleaning for her. You should be paying me more!"

Tears roll down my cheeks as a rage I haven't felt in a long time engulfs my shaking body. Who am I? For the last decade, I've been the black sheep, the child who didn't make good choices. And yet, somehow, I've ended up here in servitude, doing all the work while they look away and get on with their lives. If this is penance I need to pay for my part in the estrangement that occurred between me and my parents, then I think I have settled that debt. In bucketloads.

"There's money. I know there's money." I wait silently to see if Bel decides to change her position. If she's trying to entice me to continue doing the family's dirty work, she might as well make it worth my while.

"Okay."

My fingers run along the center panel of the shutters, pulling it down a fraction to let in a slither of sunshine. "Okay?"

"Yes, Ash, okay." Her voice cracks with her defeat. "I'll make sure you get twenty thousand when probate clears."

I click the shutters closed, hiding from the sunlight that marks my freedom. I won't be seeing it anytime soon, so I might as well get used to the dark.

Sixteen

Knowing I'm going to leave with a substantial amount of cash in my pocket at the end of all this helps. At the times when Mother is generally being annoying, I find myself repeating it like a mantra.

The money. You're doing it for the money. The money. For the money.

Unfortunately, being around Mother is exasperating ninety-nine percent of the time, and I'm starting to believe that no payout is worth the suffering. The walls are beginning to close in, and although I'm relieved, there's been no visitors to the house for weeks. I hated the dictatorial tone she took whenever she knew we would be receiving guests, bossing me to clean and tidy. The days now, however, are becoming repetitive, and a reprieve—any reprieve—would be welcome.

We've gotten into the habit of rising around eight a.m., eating, dressing, reading, and watching television. The only things that break up the monotony are the little snipes and the verbal sparring sessions that follow. After the news of another three months with the boot finally sank in, she's been reticent to do anything, making allowance only for her weekly hair appointment. And I've followed along, doing the bare minimum.

But not today. Today, I need to get out, and so does she.

The cinema complex nearby offers gold-class seating, and there's a movie I want to see that I don't think she'll mind.

"What do you say we head out for a bit later today?" I place the tray with her breakfast down and sit on the adjacent chair.

"We don't have any plans to go out." She looks over and studies me, eyebrows furrowing when she realizes I'm wearing clothes other than my grungy sweats.

"I know." I shrug. "I thought we could get out of the house. Go see a movie. That one you were talking about last week is playing, if you're interested."

"I can't do that." She picks up the container holding her pills and studies its contents. "I can't get up the stairs, and those seats are uncomfortable."

Her words are dismissive, as I knew they would be. I smile, preparing for battle. She takes a bite of her toast and is chewing slowly when I lay out my solution.

"Have you been to a gold-class cinema?"

She shakes her head, and while her mouth is full, I hurriedly explain, "They are smaller and have less seating. But the seats are bigger and probably more comfortable than the recliner you're sitting in now. There's a table between the chairs, and they bring the food and drink to you. It's very wheelchair friendly."

Her eyes light up. "What sort of food?"

"Ash, I need to go to the restroom."

Again?

She's been twice since we got here. Once on arrival and then before we were seated, and now, she needs to go when there's less than thirty minutes remaining. If I ever wondered what friends with young children went through, I now know and am now sympathetic to their plight. It's like the mystery of motherhood has been unveiled, and it's a terrible thing. Maybe Mother realizes I'll never have children and is making sure I undertake this rite of passage.

"Can't you wait until the end of the movie?" I whisper. "You're wearing your special pants."

"No, Ash. Now."

I'm thankful I reserved seats at the back of the theater, as there's plenty of space for me to maneuver her in the wheelchair. One of the two women sitting across from us looks over and shoots me a quick, almost pitying smile. I heard them speaking after they were seated and before the lights were dimmed, and I learned that their children were in daycare. I'm wishing now that my elderly child was as well.

My skills at maneuvering her wheelchair are well honed, and I manage to get her out and into the disabled restroom in record time. I'm determined to see the end of the movie, so much so that I help her onto the toilet and even tear off the toilet tissue from the roll for her. She harrumphs at being rushed but goes along with it.

I'm wheeling her down the darkened corridor with the single focus of getting back inside to watch the remainder of the movie, and I am about to enter when Mother's hand reaches back and grasps mine. I come to a complete stop, looking down to see if her bag or scarf got caught in the wheel again.

"Mary. Paul. How are you?" she says before patting my hand. "Ash, turn me around, please."

I look up to see a throng of people piling out from a set of doors, their movie obviously over. An elderly couple stops to the side of us with huge smiles on their faces.

"Elizabeth, how are you? It's so good to see you." Mary reaches down and gives Mother an awkward hug.

I back us toward the wall, out of the way of the emptying room, hoping that they have the urge to hurry this chance meeting up.

"I'm well enough. Thank you for asking," Mother says. "I'm still wearing this thing though."

Mary looks down at the boot on Mother's leg. "Yes, I heard you had a nasty fall. But wasn't that months ago? I'd have thought you'd be back on your feet by now."

Mother's tongue clicks, and I hold back a laugh. She's offended, and she's pissed, but you'd never guess if you didn't know what to look for. Paul seems to pick up on the spiteful undercurrents and appears to share my mirth. He discreetly takes a few steps back, seemingly content enough to let these women spar it out. But I'm not. I don't have time for this right now.

"Mom, we should be going. The movie's not over yet."

"Oh, how lovely for you, Elizabeth. To have family looking out for you at such a difficult time."

Even I can hear the sarcasm in her words.

"Yes, it's lovely, and she's lucky. I'm lucky. We really should be going. Be sure to come around for morning tea sometime." I wave over my shoulder, turning the chair so fast that it leaves the two busybodies eating our dust. "Bye now."

"Ash—"

"Shh, Mother. Who cares about them? Let's watch the movie."

I engage the brakes on her chair at the rear of the seating area and leave her there, stewing, while I return to the comfort of my reclined, oversize chair. The next few minutes before the credits roll are the most peaceful of my day.

When I remind myself I'm being paid to do this, it makes the whole situation a bit more palatable to bear. The entire outing was a bust. I should have realized how it would go, the same as when I take her out after her hair appointment. Why I thought this would be any different ... who knows?

It was the one thing I thought we could've done minus all of her self-absorbed, self-righteous crap. One thing. Never mind her ruining the movie for me. From the moment I'd conceived the idea, I'd made the mistake of putting my wants and needs into the mix. Maybe I'm the selfish one, hoping to steal a few moments of normalcy or pseudo freedom among this continuous, worthless existence that is my life. I should have known better. I should have realized sooner that anything entailing my mother involves nothing other than her.

Her wants.

Her needs.

Her fucking shit.

"I'm cold. Where's my clean nightdress?"

She had an accident on the way home, which required us to have an unscheduled shower. The second shower followed the accident after dinner. I'm so thankful for Joel's suggestion to have some disposable gloves handy because I would hate to be touching this with my naked hands. All she had while we were out was popcorn and soda and then some soup and toast at dinner. I'm at a loss as to where all of this ... shit has come from.

"Ash—"

"Just give me a second, Mom," I yell into the toilet bowl, taking my frustrations out on the white ceramic with the brush.

Water flicks onto my face, and I quickly wipe it with the sleeve on my arm, trying not to think about the germs and whether any got up my nose.

"This is so fucking gross," I mutter to myself, standing.

I enter the room to find Mother shivering on the edge of her bed with only a clean diaper on. The wheeled walker is locked in front of her while she waits. I let her walk in from the bathroom without her boot, so I could get a start on cleaning the mess. I'm trying to stay clinical and treat this as a job, but it's hard to separate out the year's history with this woman. Her spitefulness is contagious.

"You could have gotten it yourself." I stomp over to the dresser and notice I'm still wearing the gloves as I pull open a drawer and retrieve her pajamas. I don't care. I throw the item in her direction and watch as it lands beside her.

She tsk-tsks me, reprimanding what she perceives as me throwing a tantrum. But it's not me who's acting out. In this scenario, I'm the overworked, overtired, and underappreciated caregiver, dealing with a petulant and impatient child. The role reversal is complete, and I have the dirty diapers to prove it.

The nightdress is on, but she hasn't pulled it fully down in the rear, leaving her back exposed. Her hand reaches out in my direction, holding the plastic bottle of moisturizing cream. "Can you rub some lotion onto my back?"

There's not enough money in the world that could be considered a fair and reasonable reimbursement for the events of today, especially the last few hours. I'm at the stage where I want to call my sister and tell her she can keep the money because I'm done. It's nothing more than a bribe, I've come to realize. Hush money to keep me silent and to carry on with the job no one else wants. I look between my latex-covered hands and hers, contemplating my response.

Fuck it.

Pettiness appears to be the new norm.

"Of course, Mother."

The white salve squeezes out effortlessly, and I use it to coat her back with small, circular strokes. My nose screws up in disgust as I continue to spread the liquid, thankful for the gloves offering the separation between our skin. She sighs with contentment and rocks her body back into my hands.

"That feels so much better."

I almost barf.

I hate touching her.

"Can you ru—"

"I'm done, Mom. You'll need to do it yourself," I huff and return to the bathroom to gather up the soiled towels and garments to wash.

The smell is pungent, and my eyes water as I unfurl the items into the washing machine. I carefully peel the gloves off to dispose of them before setting the cycle and reaching for the bottle of Clorox. The strong chlorine-like odor overpowers the rancidness of the load and burns the back of my throat.

"So gross," I mutter, washing my hands in the kitchen sink before wiping down both the counter and basin with the all-purpose disinfectant spray. "So fucking gross."

My head throbs, and an ache forms behind my forehead. I open the cabinet door, hiding all of the medication to pull out the Tylenol. My fingers graze the top of the bottle of Lortab. Google searches I did after the doctor prescribed it said it contained paracetamol and hydrocodone—a strong painkiller in the right doses. Mother's dose is relatively low to help with pain but mainly to help her sleep.

I really need sleep tonight.

Before I realize it, the pill is sitting on my tongue. The bitterness of the coating mixes with my saliva, and I have a second to contemplate my course of action. Swallow or spit. I twist the tap and place my head under the faucet's stream, gulping down the pill with a mouthful of cold water.

I return to Mother's room with a glass or water and her own painkiller. I hold them out to her.

"What's the large pill? I've already taken my Lipitor with dinner."

"Huh." The white oblong tablet does appear to be similar to her atorvastatin—or Lipitor—that she takes every evening for cholesterol. It would be a reasonable assumption to confuse the two if you didn't know what you were looking at or your eyesight was not one hundred percent. "It's the sleeping pill the doctor prescribed."

"I don't want to take that. What if I have another bowel movement and don't wake up for it?" She pushes my offering away.

"That won't happen," I say, exasperated.

"How do you know? You don't. I don't need it." She lies back, crossing her arms, and glares at me.

If she doesn't take the pill, she'll stay up the entire night, worrying about whether she's going to poop her pants again. Which means she'll be calling out to me every time she needs to pass wind, thinking that it could be something more than just flatulence. I really don't want to spend my night dealing with this.

I'm tired, and I just want to sleep.

"Just take the pill, so you can get some rest—"

"No—"

"Take the pill, Mom." My voice is low and contains a bite that has her blinking back tears.

She sits up on one elbow and reaches out with the other hand. I drop the pill into it and watch as she swallows. She lies back down, and I pull the covers up as she settles back into the pillow.

"Good night, Mother."

A bony hand snatches mine before I get a chance to turn and leave. "Thanks for the day out. I appreciate you and all that you do for me."

Looking down at her, I can't tell if she means what she's saying or if it's part of an act. Something appeasing for the harsh tone I used, so she can manipulate me into feeling guilty. It's either that or part of her nightly prayers, seeking forgiveness. Thanking me as a way to absolve her daily sins.

ALL FOR MOTHER

"I love you, Ash. Good night," she whispers, fingers unfurling and eyelids fluttering closed.

I smile, my mind starting to float, and wonder if she'd still appreciate me, love me, if she knew she was lying and percolating in shitty-toilet-water-tainted lotion.

Seventeen

"Ow. It's itching again."

She doesn't need to be in today. Not really. It's my fault we're here, as I was the one who rubbed cream on her back, using latex gloves, knowing full well she was allergic. In truth, I'd forgotten about her allergy in the moment, but since I used soiled gloves, I'd expect her to have some sort of a reaction regardless.

"I know. We'll get it sorted soon."

The nasty rash didn't take long to form and cause discomfort. I found some cortisone cream among all of her medication and knew while it would work, it would be easier to come in and get it seen. Both my reasons are selfish. I knew she'd refuse to believe the rash was innocuous and easy to treat—me not being a medical professional and all. Having her see the doctor means I won't have to put up with her passive-aggressiveness while I treat it. I also want to see Joel.

I'm almost certain Mother was on her way to working out what the rash was from, but I used all my newfound manipulative skills to blur her memory and blamed it on the cinema seating. I told her I should've listened when she said she didn't want to go to see a movie, made out as if it were my fault. Blaming myself and praising her in the same breath worked. Her eyebrows scrunched up in thought, and those thin lips, normally housing a scowl, pursed so tight that they turned white for a fraction of a second before she decided my story had merit.

It's a win for me. Not only did I outmaneuver her, but my one act of sabotage also struck any future cinematic outings off the list and got us into the doctor's office ... so I could see Joel.

A melodic tune sounds our arrival as I propel through the doorway. He's behind the counter, talking to the receptionist, and smiles at our entrance, eyes lingering a fraction longer than needed before going back to his immediate task. A lightness enters my body, and I sigh in relief. I'm happy he's on shift and hope I'll be able to spend a few fleeting moments in his presence. The day or two needed to treat the skin condition will be painful but totally worth it on so many levels.

I position her, so she can watch the small mounted screen in the corner, playing medical-related infomercials continuously. Let her study up and be brainwashed into whatever the pharmaceutical companies want her to believe, to fix side effects of certain drugs with more medication. An endless loop of chemically induced problems. She generally buys into all of this, convinced there's a cure-all pill that will do exactly that. I settle back and observe the waiting area, biding my time.

We're asked to wait in one of the consulting rooms, and a nurse comes in, asks a few questions, and does all of the preliminary checks for the doctor. I shrug and feign concern when the rash is discussed but can't help but notice how angry the welts have become on her back. Latex and feces do not look to be a pleasant combination.

"It started itching this morning." Mother tells her story from the beginning when the doctor finally joins us. Everything from the movie to her accident. Her hypochondria kicks in, and she rambles on, weaving conspiracy theories about all sorts of things. "I woke up, it was uncomfortable, and here we are."

ALL FOR MOTHER

He lifts the back of her shirt and gingerly runs his fingers over the scaly red rash before going to the sink and washing his hands. "It appears to be a contact allergy. Nothing sinister that cortisone cream and an antihistamine won't fix over a few days."

I remain silent, staring at a spot on the wall over the doctor's head, knowing exactly what she was in contact with. My cheeks burn as I think about how frustrated I was with her last night and how childish it was of me to do what I did. My pettiness in the moment has achieved nothing but more work for me.

"It says in your file that you're allergic to latex. This is correct, isn't it, Mrs. Doyle?"

"Yes."

I shift uncomfortably in my seat as Mother answers him simply. For once, she doesn't start babbling with some origin story or theory to her latex allergy. I can't meet the doctor's gaze and expect it when he directs the next question to me.

"Were you wearing latex gloves last night?"

His eyes hold a look of compassion, but his words have me squirming, as if I were being interrogated under a bright light. He's, of course, referring to the diarrhea episode Mother described and me cleaning it.

"Yes," I answer softly, shame coursing through my veins.

"Well, there you go. Mystery solved."

Mother splutters as her mind tries to follow the conversation. Her hearing aids are in, and so far this morning, she hasn't feigned any auditory difficulties, so I wait, wondering if she'll piece it together, as the doctor did.

"I'm sorry, Mother. It was an accident. I didn't know."

"Never mind," the doctor says, handing me the paper scripts and patting me on the arm. "This will have it all cleared up within a few days. When you're in the pharmacy, picking up the cream, ask for some alternative latex-free gloves. That'll stop this from happening again."

I nod, thankful that neither of them has pieced together the extent of my guilt. That it only took a fraction of a second to make the decision to cause her discomfort, cause her pain. I shuffle my feet, annoyed with myself now, thinking I should've treated this at home instead of bringing her in to have it documented on file. This visit might fuel Mother's doubt in my ability to care for her, as she will undoubtedly weave it into a tragic tale to my sister. Even though the money has been at the forefront of my mind since Bel agreed to pay me, I forgot how easily they could take the promise of it away. My pettiness could be my undoing.

"Of course."

The corridor is deserted when I wheel Mother out to the accounting desk. I apply the brakes and hastily make an excuse to allow me to disappear to the restroom for a few stolen moments. After splashing water on my face, I study my reflection in the mirror. The dim lighting overhead does not hide the dark rings under my eyes or the limpness of my hair.

I am a mess. A geriatric-abusing—more accurately, a geriatric-abused—mess.

No money is worth this, but I am almost there. Almost to the finish line. To my payday.

I exit the restroom with a resolve to do better. Head down, I don't see Joel until I practically bump into him.

"Hey you," he says, grabbing my arm and pulling me through a door. "I've missed you. How's your mom?"

The quiet click of the door hides us away from prying eyes and the brightness of the corridor. The room is a small supply room of sorts, shelves of surplus first aid supplies, protective equipment, and medication. He spins me around and traps me against the wall, and I tip my head back, looking at the ceiling as I confess my crime.

"Mother's rash is my fault. I was wearing latex gloves when I rubbed lotion on her back yesterday."

He laughs. "Shit happens. It's not the end of the world."

I don't admit that shit does happen and the lotion was laced with it. I don't think he'd be laughing if he knew the whole story.

"Yes," I mumble. "It was an accident."

He leans in and kisses me. It's tentative and soft, and my body relaxes against him. The anxiety resulting from today's visit is washed away, and I'm absorbed in this moment.

"Oops," he says, pulling back to check an incoming message. "I have to go."

"Oh."

"It'll be okay." His hand moves up to cup the side of my face. The warmth of his palm feels like home, reminding me of lazy mornings and fireplaces. "I've got to go, but we should catch up later this week. Your mom will be fine. You're amazing and doing a wonderful job. Remember that."

He leaves me with the lingering imprint of his hand and lips, and I take a minute to compose myself. Joel's right. Mother is fine, and I'm doing my best.

The boxes of prescription drugs on the shelf catch my eye. Before thinking too much about it, I pocket one and leave.

Mother's lucky to have me caring for her. Not many people would be able to put up with her under the current circumstances for as long as I have. She's hard to live with, and I should be forgiven for some of my petty actions.

I just need to be more careful.

Eighteen

Joel texted me sometime this afternoon, but I was too busy, hurrying around with Mother, and missed the message when it came through. He wanted to know if I could join him tonight for drinks at the wine bar in town.

Of course I can't.

It's a forty-five-minute round-trip on a normal day with light traffic, and today is Friday. And then there's ... her.

We've already been out and visited the salon. While she was being made up to prom-queen status, I finished off a six-pack of chocolate-filled donuts. The only thing that would've made those scrumptious delights better was if the white-powdered heaven sprinkled on top were ground codeine. Or Valium. It's so nice when I don't have to think ... or feel. But I can't afford to slip up out in public, especially when she's with me.

I look across the hall and see her lazing in the sunroom, seat reclined and leg rest raised. She was cold, and I already draped the red knitted throw across her feet and legs. For whatever reason, she's been complaining of the coolness lately, overdressing and shivering whenever she lowers her britches to relieve herself. Although she's supposedly freezing, it doesn't stop her from demanding a bowl of ice cream with hot fudge, as if the hot chocolate topping will scare away the chills.

She asked for three scoops of the French vanilla bean, but I decide to only give her two with a small amount of the fudge. I could've given her more, but the heated darkness is so good that I spoon most of it in my mouth. It would anger her if she knew the amount of sugar I've consumed today. I'd hear all the stories of how her brother's sister-in-law's second cousin's son's stepsister was a diabetic and died from sugar poisoning. As if that's a thing. But she'd tell me it was true and that I was following in those obese footsteps of the distant relatives—to live either a long and lonely life as a fat, spouseless loser or die an early death as an unwedded failure. I always end up being overweight and unmarried in her cautionary tales. Totally Mother of the Year material.

The ice cream is consumed rapidly and with the level of vigor I'd prefer to see put into self-care or even mobility. Despite the speed in which she devours it, the ice cream still manages to soften, allowing her shaking hands to spill droplets on her clothing. I knew the ice cream was a bad idea. For such a supposedly small treat, the potential to create over an hour's extra work this evening is all too real, as she'll demand to be changed and for her soiled garments to be treated immediately so as to not stain. She'd probably stay up to make sure I did it too.

Perhaps she won't notice the off-color marks. I can only hope the wet spots don't leak through to her skin, so she'll feel it. If it doesn't, I might be in the clear.

Maybe I could go tonight. If I convince her to retire early, she'd potentially be down for the count to allow me to steal a few secreted hours. Especially if I can get her to take the Trazodone. Enough time to share a drink and be social. It would all hinge on whether she's going to claim to be in pain and to not be able to sleep—all the more reason she should take the medication. On the nights when that happens, she likes to call out every hour to ask me to remove a blanket, add a blanket, pull the curtain, or turn the fan on.

ALL FOR MOTHER

The days and nights have been blending together. It feels like only yesterday when we were at the doctor's office for the latex rash. Or was it the review of the break? Yesterday could have been the day she fell and broke her leg and ruined my tomorrow. That's how long this nightmare has lasted ... an eternity. I'm a rodent caught on a wheel and too tired to look for an exit.

I sniff and wipe the end of my nose, annoyed with the allergies I've been fighting lately. Antihistamines haven't been helping; they just make my mouth dry.

Watching her live her best life with me at her beck and call hollows out my insides, allowing the fire of dissent to burn fiercely. It spurs me into action because *I* deserve to live my best life.

"Mom? Do you think a glass of wine or a whiskey will help warm you up?"

I look at my watch and calculate the minutes I have to get her to bed and give me enough time to shower and make it to the bar. Alcohol might be my best answer, but I need to tread carefully. Sometimes, she's up for a small, naughty nip, but other times, she likes to chastise me. It all depends on whether the voices speaking to her tonight are wearing the red cloak or the white.

She pushes the empty bowl to the edge of the side table and looks over to me. "That might be nice." The corners of her lips lift to form an awkward smile. "These old bones are rather cold. It can't hurt."

"No, it can't. What would you prefer—whiskey or wine?" My hands tremble slightly, and I hide them behind my back, wondering myself which of the two would be better at concealing the taste of her sleeping medication.

"Wine. Do we have any red?" She picks up the remote and changes the channel, finding a rerun of *Wheel of Fortune* to monopolize her attention.

"I'll go look," I say in my most amiable tone.

While she's preoccupied with the television, I quickly pick up her pill cup with the discarded bowl. She hasn't taken her evening medication yet, and there's time for me to switch some of them out. I pull out my cell phone on the way to the kitchen for what feels like the hundredth time to recheck the message from Joel and send off a reply.

Tonight is going to be just what *my doctor* ordered.

Opening the cabinet, I study the lined bottles and retrieve those I'll need along with the pill cutter. Lortab, codeine, and Valium. Lining the codeine on the mini guillotine, I splice it in half and then in half again before switching her heart meds out for the newly cut quarter tab. The Lortab replaces the Lipitor, and my hand stills, holding both the Trazodone and the low-dose aspirin, grimacing at the size difference. I don't think I can swap these out; she might notice. The Valium is smaller, but it's also not a good fit.

Metal clangs as I rifle through a drawer, searching for the sharpened paring knife. The wooden butcher block provides the sturdy surface for my attempt to whittle the edges of the valium down to a circumference similar to the aspirin. It doesn't work the way I want it to, and my palms hit the counter in frustration.

Hands lay flat on either side of the cutting board, my splayed fingers stark against the backdrop of the dark gray laminate countertop. I study them, long fingers with nails bitten down to the quick and angry red skin around most of the edges.

What am I doing?
What has she turned me into?

I never asked to be in this situation, to be her companion and caregiver. The guilt from the few times I've either forced drugs onto her or crushed them into her food is still there. Me doing that took away her voice. Her power. Her rights. I know it's not justified, but she's proven time and time again to be incapable of making rational decisions related to her medication. If she applied common sense and looked around once in a while to see

ALL FOR MOTHER

what was really going on and how her decisions and attitude affected others—namely me—she might realize how selfish and ridiculous she was being. Not to mention, how her comfort levels would benefit from taking the prescribed medication when she felt pain.

The inside of my cheek smarts with the molars biting down hard enough to draw blood. It's a complex and difficult decision for me to know what's right. Legally, she can have all of these. She has the prescriptions, and from the doctor's perspective, she should be taking advantage of them during this healing process. But if she doesn't want to and refuses to take them ...

I promised myself I'd try to be better, but I don't want to end up with any regrets. No regrets for actions taken or not taken. Or for pursuing a few moments away from her. Moments with someone else who actually cares ... with Joel.

But she's such a bitch. Her mental state is deteriorating. The dementia eats away fragments of her mind daily, stripping her of any goodness, highlighting the negative traits, and magnifying all of the unresolved psychological crap from her past. Mother is a bitch, and dementia is her mistress. It seems to have lifted up the mask that shrouded her inner character to show who she actually has been all along.

The knife makes quick work, scraping the misshapen Valium and all the scattered chunks and powder into a plastic Ziploc bag along with the cut codeine. Squinting, I check the marking on the oblong white pill, making sure to put the right one into Mother's cup before returning to the sitting room with her glass of wine.

"Here you go," I say, placing everything down beside her.

She adjusts the recliner, and with gnarly fingers, she picks the corner of the woolen blanket. "Can you take this? It's itching my legs."

It takes great restraint to hold in my annoyance, but I do as she asked, wondering if I'll be replacing it in twenty minutes. If I have my way, she'll be sleeping in ten minutes.

"I'll just leave it here. If you get cold again, you can grab it yourself." I know she won't, and I don't really know why I bother. The itchiness is a lie, some deranged story used as justification to ask for its removal. It all makes sense in her mind. "I'm going to clean the kitchen. I'll be back soon to help you to bed."

She waves me away, and I leave her to her television. And her pills and wine.

I ignore the kitchen, and my feet take me to my room, where I fall on top of a pile of clean clothes on the mattress. As I take measured breaths in and out, a numbness overtakes my limbs. I'm so exhausted, both mentally and physically. I could sleep like this. Cadenced clicks from the fan above lulls me into a sense of the in-between. I'm in my body, but I'm not.

Reluctantly, I push up and sort through the washing to find clean jeans for tonight. Fingers brush against parchment, and I roll on my back, raising it above my head to catch the light. They're my drawings from this afternoon. So much of my current mood has been absorbed by the black pencil scratches. A deeper darkness hiding beneath each line.

Showering, I allow the water to wash away the doldrums and prepare for my night. I keep my attire low-key, pulling a stained oversize sweater on to throw Mother off the scent. She doesn't need to know I'm going out.

I don't want her to know.

I don't want the questions or the judgment.

"Mom, are you ready for—"

The chair is in full recline, and her head is lolled to the side. Slack jaw open.

"Shit."

ALL FOR MOTHER

Soft, rumbling snorts accompany exhaled breaths, competing with buzzers from the now-playing *Jeopardy!* rerun. I carefully nudge her, take the remote from her hand, and turn the television off.

"Mom. Wake up."

She startles away with a grunt and a fart. Flatulence is one thing I don't want to catch when I get older. Her eyes look up, fear flashing through them for a second before being replaced by confusion.

"It's time for bed. Let me help you. Do you want me to wheel you on the walker, or can you make it yourself?"

She takes a few seconds to think it over, eyelashes fluttering as she looks around, trying to grasp the situation. "You can push me." Her voice is low, and she slurs her words.

I tell myself it's because she's just been roused and not entirely cognizant and that it's not from the combination of her medication and alcohol. Her feet drag on the carpet as I push her to the bathroom before helping her onto the commode. Robotic actions tell the truth about how many times this routine has been played out over the past months, and within minutes, I have her lying in a fresh diaper on her bed and am pulling up the covers. Her nightgown still sports the discolored area from her dessert, but she never noticed, and I never brought it to her attention.

Tonight has been easy, and I'm relieved.

I tuck in the edges of the sheets under the mattress, remembering a time when she did the same for me. Too much time has passed since those innocent days of childhood. The earth turns, and time has molded me as much as it has molded her. For better or for worse.

She's so peaceful when asleep, her tongue unable to spit its vitriol. I'm halfway to the door, mentally going through the checklist for my rendezvous with Joel, when I stop. Hair prickles uneasily at the nape of my neck, and I have the absurd feeling of being watched. Turning slowly,

I study the room, wondering if my subconscious is trying to tell me I've forgotten something.

My eyes meet hers.

"Good night, Ash."

I swallow. "Good night, Mother."

Nineteen

The sun breaks through the canopy, casting a surreal luminescence around the trees outside my window. I woke due to the rain. Its dance on the roof with an even cadence entices me to stay in bed. If it wasn't for the lack of darkness, I might. The growing brightness means I should get up and see to Mother.

Should but I don't want to.

Leaves glisten, reflecting the morning light, and birds call out to each other with such a mesmerizing sweet song that lulls me back to the land of nod.

Almost.

Not quite.

I wish.

This morning's gift is something I don't want to take for granted. I can't. Although the windows are closed, the crisp, clean, pine-soaked air from outside somehow permeates through. The particles of freshness meet my nose somehow, allowing me to taste it, bringing forth memories from my youth when I would run and play in the rain. I close my eyes, wanting this moment to last, as I imagine myself frolicking in the golden light, free as a gypsy. Free as the air itself. Free to live my life as I want. To wave my rainbow flag of uniqueness and dance with unicorns. The freedom of my youth that I no longer have due to aging and unwanted responsibilities. The freedom that was soured by my family's disowning me.

Yet I find myself here. A second chance spindled with barbed wire.

My lips upturn slightly, and I rub the sleep from my eyes. It's going to be a long day; I can already tell. Not enough sleep and a throb behind my temple, reminders of my secret tryst last night.

Well-worn sheets trap my legs in their knotted chaos as I roll to my side to hit snooze on the alarm that's broken the silence. It's time for the day to start. As much as I want to stay in the cocoon of warmth—reveling in happy, almost-mystical memories—I can't. It won't take long before the melancholy of past and present sins engulfs the joyful thoughts and memories. I really don't want to taint those. Besides, the necessary chores of servitude need to be completed before *she* wakes, complains, and sucks more of my life from me.

As expected, my mood sours somewhat with this thought and even more so when the sun moves behind a cloud, cutting its rays from my magical view. The otherworldliness disappears, and the normal mundane filter of my life returns in its stead.

Reluctantly, I rise and change into something that can pass for comfort. The house's negativity cloys my frame of mind, and I take the time to splash water on my face, brush my teeth, and comb the knots from my hair. Self-care is not really for me; it's for the visitors and neighbors or even the grocery-store worker ... if I get the chance to leave today. I don't care much for my looks, maybe to spite her Southern sensibilities that suggest one should always look their best. But it's never been that way for me. Not in the sense to make me feel better about myself. I use what I can from my arsenal to mask everything within my mind and soul and only take the time to outwardly appear as I should—clothes, hair, face. A disguise to cover the reality, as much as I fight it, that my zest for life is being

ALL FOR MOTHER

bled dry and given to this aged wraith who doesn't appreciate me. Much less understand or know me. Her own child.

Using the stealth of a ninja, I softly tread to Mother's room and carefully push the door ajar. She's in the same position I left her in last night—on her back, fingers poking out and gripping the top of her covers. The duvet rises and lowers with a slow, rhythmic flow. Each jagged inhalation raspy and accompanied by a barely discernable whistling sound. If it wasn't for the movement, she might be mistaken for an entombed, shriveled vampire elder, waiting for a willing victim to provide their lifeblood in exchange for youth and mortality. The same vampire from my cautionary tales of decades prior.

I quietly retreat, hoping not to disturb her, and make my way to the kitchen for Advil and coffee. The ibuprofen will still my headache, and the coffee will hopefully perk me up enough to deal with the day. Lined pill bottles resting beside a few pharmacy-marked boxes in the cupboard call to me, asking to come out and play. In a trancelike state, I oblige.

With skills to rival any medieval alchemist, I place my preferred drugs in the mortar and pestle and grind them down to a fine powder. My symptoms comprise of headache, allergies, lethargy, and a good measure of *I'm over this shit, and I don't really give a fuck*, but it's the last one that has me adding a codeine tab to the mix. It'll help numb the pain of yet another monotonous day with Mother.

The kitchen's a mess. I didn't clean it last night, and I'm not entirely happy about the prospect of doing it today. The thought of loading the dishwasher, adding powder, and turning it on has my muscles tensing. My body's fighting the urge to do what I know needs to be done. I push some strands of hair behind an ear and decide to make toast instead. Maybe after eating, I'll have the energy or the willpower to stack the dishes.

It doesn't take long for the single piece of bread to golden. I smear a coating of salted butter and wait for it to get to the stage where it's softened and almost melted before I season it with the contents from the mortar. The chalky white particles absorb easily, and I slather a thick layer of raspberry jelly on top. The tartness of the berries disguises the acidic bitterness of the pills.

"Ash."

The voice is weak and hesitant, and she sounds like she's not quite awake, so I ignore her. Instead of running to her like I normally would, I finish brewing the coffee. The first sip is always the best, and I savor the moment with the wafts of smoky and lightly caramelized flavors, reminding me of my meeting with Joel last week. The thick blackness is heaven—

"Ash?"

Was heaven.

I place the mug down on the countertop and take a few shaky steps before regaining control of my legs and go see Mother.

"Good morning," I say overly brightly. I pull open the blinds and let the light invade the space. "It was raining earlier this morning, but it looks like it's clearing up to be a beautiful day."

Apparently, I'm now The Weather Channel. I stand over her and flick the linen out of her tight grip to pull it down the length of the bed, the scent of urine greeting me. Going through the motions, I help her up and into the bathroom. Once she's seated, I strip her of her nightgown and leave her shivering and completely naked to finish her business.

While she strains over the toilet, I remove all the bedding. Not bothering to deal with the soiled sheets, I roll them carefully into a ball and shove them on the highest shelf in the hall cupboard. Washing can be done later. Or maybe they'll dry, and I'll use them again. No one would know. Especially not her.

ALL FOR MOTHER

The grunting and whimpers quickly turn to a sigh of relief as her bowel movement reaches its final destination into the watery grave below. It's a short-lived victory, as different muscles struggle with the task of unraveling the toilet tissue needed to wipe away the mess, and the gurgles and groans let me know she's not done. Not yet anyway. I close my eyes and lean against the wall, enjoying the burst of colors behind my eyelids and the growing sense of weightlessness.

A final sob and the flush of the toilet is the signal—the daily repetitive signal—that she's done, and I return to find her struggling to push up from the seated position. Sagging skin draped over brittle bones quiver as she manages to make it halfway. I grip an arm, careful to monitor the pressure so as not to leave a bruise.

"Did you want to clean up first?" I question softly, holding her still.

Her bottom lip trembles, and she nods once while struggling to find her words. When they come, they're barely audible. "Yes, please."

She sits back down while I wet a washcloth under warm water before handing it to her. I place a clean pair of her pee pants on the counter, excuse myself, and leave her to her limited ablutions.

Stepping into her walk-in wardrobe, I let my fingers explore the textures of all of the hanging clothes. The space is as long as her room with hangers draped with finery lining each side. Some still have their sales tags attached. All of these items have been tucked away for a special event or outing. There'll never be enough time for her to wear these. Time is everyone's enemy but especially hers. These clothes represent her vain sensibilities and desire to fit into a world she'll soon leave.

What a waste.

On a whim, I pull a skirt, a shirt, and a jacket off their hangers. The colors are pretty, and they remind me of geraniums and daffodils. I lift the garments to my nose and almost choke on the faint, sickly-sweet smell of mothballs. The odor makes my head spin. It's everywhere, and the walls feel like they're slowly closing in. I need to escape.

"Here," I say, thrusting the selected clothing into her lap.

"I don't want these," she says, pushing them back toward me. The towel she has draped over her shoulders slips, and she catches it in time to pull it tighter. "Get me a nightgown, please. I'm cold. You've left me in here, freezing, for twenty minutes."

"No." I shove the items back and take a step away from her, forcing her to catch them before they fall onto the floor. "Why can't you wear them? You have so many clothes lined up in your crypt of a wardrobe, and for what?"

"I'm not wearing these. They're completely unsuitable."

"Why? Because I picked them out?"

"Because"—she swats the air in annoyance—"they're fall colors, not at all suitable for this time of year."

What the ...

"Does it really matter?"

"Yes, it does." She reaches across to place the items of clothing onto the sink, not noticing when they slide into the basin, colors on the fabric deepening as water wicks into the material.

"Oh my God! Are you serious?" I cross my arms across my body and stare at her.

"Ash, get me a nightgown." She raises her voice, using that authoritarian tone she likes to boss me around with.

It's been days since she's used it. My recent attitude of *peu importe* has caused her to be more reserved as of late.

"No!" I stamp my foot. I bend down to her level and position my face directly in front of hers, taking immense delight as she shrinks away from me. "No, I will not. You ruin all the fun. I thought it might be fun to go out today, but you know what? I don't want to anymore. I'll return your clothes to your fucking crypt."

I snatch the damp clothes and exit the room, rolling them up into a ball. They can join her filthy sheets in the hall cupboard. As an afterthought, I call over my shoulder, "I'm not your servant. Get your own fucking nightdress."

TWENTY

"Here you go." My feet trip over the carpet, and I barely manage to save the items on the tray from flying into her lap. "Oops!"

"Have you been drinking?"

An unwelcome snort erupts from me, and I desperately try to swallow down the beginning of a chuckle. Mother arches back into her chair, tilting her head to the side to study me with a frown. I quickly place her breakfast down and move to the other side of the room.

"What is—"

"I'm not feeling well," I cut her off before she can express her displeasure with my behavior or what I've brought her for breakfast. A piece of week-old buttered nut loaf bread and yesterday's leftover coffee, both heated up in the microwave. I've included some pills, and I hope they're the right ones. I wasn't paying much attention this morning when I got up and decided the best way to cure a hangover was to wash down some meds with another drink. "I think I'm coming down with something and probably just need to go lie down for a while."

I let my posture sag, push my bottom lip out, and try my best to look like a wounded puppy. At this point, I'll do anything to get away from her for a few hours. The days are too long, and being in her presence, either directly or peripherally, is just too much.

She's been acting strange lately. Very unpredictable. Still the ever-demanding and manipulative bitch, but there's something not right. She's been watching me more, and I think I've caught her a few times complaining to my sister about me.

"Okay," she says slowly. "You go rest. We can call for some takeout to be delivered later. Don't worry about me. I'm all set up now. I'll be fine for the next little bit."

I know she will be. I can't believe she's fallen for my act.

I wake with a start.

What was that?

The doorbell sounds, followed by a hesitant knock. I roll out of bed, pull on some sweats, and run my fingers through my hair in an effort to look less like I just woke up. The opaque paneling on the front door reveals a silhouette of a petite woman and not the UPS guy I was expecting.

"Can I help you?"

The abruptness of my greeting as the door swings open has the woman jumping back in surprise. She's well dressed, and she looks to be in her eighties. A healthy and agile elderly lady, unlike my mother, holding a covered glass baking dish in her hands.

"I-I was hoping to see Elizabeth?"

Narrowing my eyes, I scrutinize her in more detail. She's been here before, a friend of Mother's from church. She lives in the aged care facility over by the beach and has been championing the crusade to get Mother to join her as a permanent resident. In the immediate weeks post Father's death, Mother wasn't interested in moving anywhere. Although there's no money to pay for the move right now, I can't have Mother changing her mind. Not until I'm paid. Then, she can do what she wants.

"Miss Sandra?" I question slowly, hoping I got the name right.

Her lips thin, and her eyebrows furrow ever so slightly before she takes a big breath and forces a bright smile on her face.

"Susan," she says, correcting me. "Is Lizzy here? I'd very much like to drop this off and spend some time with her."

My hackles rise with a sense that something's not quite right. I straighten to my full height, pull my shoulders back, and look down at her. I am a giant next to this diminutive woman. She notices as well and takes a half-step to the side, all while trying to peer behind me into the house.

I can't let this woman in. I'm not entirely sure what her motives are, but I don't think they'd be favorable to me.

Under no circumstances am I going to let Sandy-Su into the house. *Why is she here?*

My ears pick up the telltale hydraulics of Mother's chair. She must have orchestrated this visit. Been expecting it. She must have been putting on the sweet-mother act when I told her I was sick. Typical. But she should have known I'd answer the door.

Mistake number one, Mother.

I'm on high alert now. Who knows what she's told this Susan to have her here, making an unannounced visit? I'm normally so good with being five steps ahead of Mother so that I control the narrative and have the upper hand when she starts talking smack to Bel. Or anyone else. I cut her off at the pass before she's even able to mount an argument or a complaint. By texting or calling Bel prior, any official report given by Mother of my incompetence or temper is diluted and paints her in a bad light and as the troublemaker. The family expects Mother's complaints.

She's old and cantankerous. But even if my past has me on thin ice, I'm still the one here, carrying out a job no one else is interested in doing.

I need to get rid of this woman. Get in front of this, regain control of the narrative. I haven't heard the click of the brakes on Mother's walker yet, so I have time.

"Mom hasn't been well lately," I say in almost a whisper, taking a step forward and closing the door behind me. As I break eye contact with her, my hand rubs my chin, and I slowly exhale with my best effort at a concerned sigh. "She's been in a lot of pain. The bones are still mending, and it's taking longer than it should. The doctor has prescribed her some pretty hard-core painkillers, and they make her erratic at times and sometimes ... manic."

Susan gasps, fingers touching her parted lips. "Really? I did not know." Her tone is disbelieving, but she leans forward, body language telling me she wants to know more.

"The family doesn't want it widely known," I say conspiratorially, knowing she's going to love this next bit of my tale. "But with my father's death and then the fall ... she's become a bit unhinged. It's why I'm still here, making sure she doesn't do anything silly. I have to monitor the pills, you know."

"Of course." She nods, eyes softening. "Am I able to see her?"

"She's asleep right now. She was in pain earlier and asked for some of her meds. I'm afraid she fell asleep not long after. I could wake her, but it's probably better if she gets her rest. I hope you understand."

"I see."

Her wheels are spinning, and I'm not sure if I've totally convinced her. I can see her internal battle and decide to go in for the kill.

"Mom has your number. I can call you when she's feeling more like herself. The doctor said she should only

ALL FOR MOTHER

be on these meds for a few more weeks while she has the moon boot on, and we're all hoping she'll spring back to her normal self after that. I think it's just a little rough patch."

She smiles, and I know I've won this round when she hands over the food.

"That sounds great." She reaches out and gently pats my arm. "Your mother is so lucky to have you. I know it's been hard, but keep up the good work."

"Yes, ma'am," I say, watching her descend the stairs and make her way to the car parked on the curb. "Mom will be sad she missed you. Thanks for the food."

With a final wave as she drives away, I sigh and reenter the house.

That was a close call.

My eyes slowly adjust to the dimness inside. It's lucky Susan didn't come in to be greeted by this mess. Empty UPS and Amazon boxes are piled in the corner, almost toppling the dead potted plant. I might have forgotten to water it over the last few weeks. Letters and junk mail are mixed up in the dust of the hall table. As long as I send the bills to Bel for payment, I don't really care about the rest. But Susan turning up has me thinking that maybe I need to tidy up this area to be a bit more presentable.

But not now.

First, I need to deal with Mother. She's up to something, and although I can't work out what, I aim to get to the bottom of it.

There's no sound coming from the back room. No click-clacking of the walker or drag of the boot, nor is there even any whimpering or sounds of loud breathing.

I place Susan's dish on the dining table and lift the corner of the aluminum cover to stick my fingers in. My mouth waters as the flavors of chicken and mushroom hit my tongue. Leaving the casserole where it is, I retrieve a book from one of the boxes by the front door before silently walking to Mother's sunroom, where I watch from the doorway as she attempts to stand.

"Phone," I say, holding my hand out.

"What?" she replies, confused and looking around me. She's sitting on the edge of her chair with the wheeled walker in front of her. With a frustrated sigh, she pushes it away and sits back, twisting her body to watch the door.

"Where's your phone?"

She clenches her jaw and raises her chin. "I don't know."

A small movement gives her away, and I laugh.

"You're such a child," I say, pushing her arm to the side and retrieving it. I scroll through the entries and confirm she made the call to Susan this morning after I left her to her devices.

"Where's Susan?"

I ignore her question. It should be obvious; Susan isn't here. A pillow on the seat across from her recliner falls to the floor when I sit down. We need to get a few things straight, and I need to have her in the right frame of mind. These little head games we've been playing with each other can't escalate. They can't. I need her compliant and not wanting to undertake a coup to replace me with someone else or some facility. Not yet anyway. As soon as her boot is gone, all bets are off. But for now, I need to come across as dutiful, and she needs to be as accommodating as she can be.

"Please don't call anyone and ask them to come around." My voice is calm, nonthreatening. I'm doing a good job of appearing unruffled.

"Why not? It's my house. Or did you forget?"

One one thousand, two one thousand ...

"I know, Mom. It's your house. What I am trying to say is, if you can, discuss it with me first to make sure we have things in place to entertain people. That's all."

She's looking at me strangely, and I completely understand why. I have vague recollections of things I might have said and done in her presence, so this pleasant and relaxed person before her now might seem like a stranger.

"Susan couldn't stay. She wished she could but had to be somewhere else. I asked her to come around next week, if that's all right with you? She did drop off this book for you." I reach across the space between us and drop the paperback into her lap. "I'm sorry I wasn't feeling well this morning, but the few hours' rest I got helped. Do you still want to order some takeout and watch a movie after lunch, or do you want me to make some soup and sandwiches?"

She fingers the book, flicking at the pages. "Soup and sandwiches will be fine."

"Okay, done." I clap my hands on my thighs, making her jump. "I pulled some meat out of the freezer earlier. I'll make chicken casserole for dinner. That will be nice, won't it?"

Her nod is hesitant, but it's there.

My head is throbbing, and my mouth is parched from all of this talking. With the situation now under control and crisis averted, I prepare her a PB & J and add hot water to our chicken noodle packet soup mix, complete with a crushed Valium. I'm looking forward to sleeping the afternoon's babysitting duties away with less of a headache.

TWENTY-ONE

The alarm goes off, marking the start to another day. I set it to wake me earlier, wanting some precious time to myself. It's dark out, a ridiculous time to be getting up, but the solitude will be worth it.

Dressed in clothes from yesterday, I soundlessly enter the kitchen, choosing to illuminate the space with the stovetop light. Shadows dance around the corners of the room, taunting me. Tendrils of darkness looking to grab hold and bring me down. Depending on Mother's state of mind when she wakes, they very well might succeed.

Our constant to and fro mimics the changing tides. The highs, with the gentle sway of movement, cover the sand and rock. Her mind is full, with the ability to float from one point to another, wits intact. At the low, she's exposed; debris becomes trapped in the vulnerable crevices, affecting her mental faculties as judgment and reasoning are washed away. If plastic on beaches kill marine life through suffocation and choking, I can only imagine what the effect of such toxic exposure has on her brain.

That's the curse of dementia—slowly poisoning her brain, destroying neurons, disrupting signals by depriving cognizant thought. Tantrums and childlike behavior leap out during these episodes, where cutting remarks are all too soon forgotten ... by her.

Never by me.

The residue from her imprecations settle in my bones, and it takes all my willpower to control the emotions they elicit from me. Sometimes, I succeed, and sometimes, I don't.

The nutty aroma pricks my olfactory senses, providing the reason and want for solitude. With my palms heated, wrapped around the weighted mug, my lips part in anticipation of the warm, dark liquid. I've barely raised the hot coffee to my mouth when the summons comes from the back of the house.

"Ash?"

I look down at my drink and sigh. Closing my eyes, I pretend not to have heard and start the count, trying to guess how long it'll be before the next call comes.

One.
Just five minutes more ...
Two.
Please, just another five ...
Three.
If I'm quiet, she'll go back to sleep ...
Four.
Mmm. Coffee ...

"Ash!"

My eyes open, and I'm jarred out of the blissful moment by the high-pitched cry. The first call sounded like a question—soft, tentative, wavering on the end—as though she were testing, determining if I was awake. The second was an order, my name strung out with an edge, bordering on hysterical.

Despite my intent on remaining as quiet as possible, the scent of my morning goodness was more than likely the culprit that wafted down the corridor and through the cracks and crevices of her door, revealing my presence. Announcing my activities and by default sending out a notification that I was awake and ready for the day.

Such a lie.

ALL FOR MOTHER

"Ash!" The demand is abundantly clear. Short, sharp, gruff tone hinting at thinly veiled annoyance and anger.

The steam rises from my tabled cup, taunting me. It's not fair. I just took a seat ... and it's fucking early. Too early to be dealing with her wants and needs.

I don't want to go to her. I want this time, this space, for me. More importantly, I think I need it. I'm exhausted, which seems hilarious since I've been sitting on my ass for the good part of the last few weeks. Or has it been months? The mental strength has seeped away.

It could have been years, and it won't change the fact that she's calling out to me. Right. Now. Right when I want to have a small piece of calm. And my fucking coffee.

But of course, I'll go to her.

Not out of choice, but out of necessity. Why the hell she's up at this ungodly hour has me baffled as much as I'm annoyed, but I need to know. Casting a final longing look at my morning caffeine fix, I head her way.

She's dressed, and she has decided to take breakfast at the table in the kitchen like a normal person. I'm both pleased and frustrated. Her being in here doesn't make me feel any less like the servant. It just saves me from walking from one room to the other with her food.

I don't want to talk to her. It's too early for the verbal combat to begin. I wanted a bit of time to myself to get my brain on the wavelength that automatically filters the bullshit.

My body works on autopilot.

Coffee cup.

Coffee.

Add some milk.

Bread in the toaster.

Plate, knife, butter, and the strawberry jelly.

Not the raspberry or wild berries. Only ever the strawberry.

Pills out and in the cup.

Water.

Napkin.

I place everything in front of her without a word. It shouldn't take more than the two minutes for the toast to pop up. A dense silence fills the space as she fidgets, and I wait, holding my breath, for the ping from the toaster.

I need to refill her scripts today. It's a joyless task, but it'll get me out of the house for a few precious hours. An escape, one that doesn't need to come with any justification. One that I've already planned to coincide with Joel's lunch.

The plastic container filled with the paperwork makes an almost-inaudible sound as it kisses the countertop. It's enough for her to sit up and take note. Her beady eyes watch my every move as I carefully take stock of the almost-empty bottles and find the prescriptions that match.

"Hand me that bottle," she says, gesturing toward the over-the-counter stool softener. "That's the red ones you normally give me, isn't it?"

"Yes." My voice is flat and monotone.

I sigh. I can already tell this morning will not be a good one. I just need to make it through until it's time for my reprieve.

Twenty-Two

Buzzing.

A swarm of busy bees buzzes around my head. In my head. I'm cognizant enough to realize they're not there literally, of course. The knowledge doesn't stop me from swatting at empty space before resting my head against the wall, the coolness affording me much-needed yet temporary relief. Lights flash behind my eyelids due to the increased pressure applied to keep them closed. The knocking against the wall is hollow, much like the head striking it.

I can't do this anymore. I just can't.

The clean scent from my favorite ripped tee of an '80s popular band is inhaled deeply before the loud exhalation escapes. It's vintage. I've owned it for over a decade, and its sentimental value is more than the reality of it being worthless and not of much more use than as a dishrag. The well-worn material provides comfort and caresses my body like the arms of a caring lover. Or, as I look down at her wretched body, could it be like the arms of a caring mother?

Ha. That'd be the day. I chortle and hurriedly wipe the spittle from my face.

She startles, eyes blinking rapidly with the invasion of the room's artificial light. She's been doing that as of late with my off-the-wall comments and reactions. I'm in my head too much, and she can't appreciate what's funny. Not that she'd be overly happy with most of my thoughts. Humor is not one of her strengths. At this point in her life, she's lacking a lot in the strength department.

She's lying in the same position I left her in hours earlier. Every morning is the same. It's an endless nightmare from which I am unable to extricate myself from. It doesn't matter whether I get drunk or high; it's always the same. There's no escaping it.

Her bony fingers pull at the sheets, bringing them to her chin, and it starts—complaints about the temperature. I knew this would be coming when her teeth started chattering last night, so I adjusted the thermostat after she refused an extra blanket. I didn't tell her this though, so her being cold is all in her head.

Completely in her head.

As I am in mine.

Her saying she's cold is because she thinks she's meant to be. To her knowledge, the ambient temperature is the sixty-six it's normally set to. But I switched it last night to seventy to chase off the chills. I don't know why I bothered.

Her whining at the moment is no different to the nonsensical crap she likes to spurt out most of the time because she believes it's the proper response or the suitable reaction to a situation. I think she forgot a long time ago that she's human and she can afford to have her own opinions or thoughts instead of sprouting whatever crap certain Southern ladies of stature deem suitable. To the outside world, she puts on this facade to try and seem worldly or be seen as compassionate, to not ruffle any feathers. It's a generational sham to be sure but one she refuses to do without.

But here, in the house, with me as her only companion, she drops the good manners and is downright rude and inappropriate. This is who she really is. But only when others are not watching. I have no proof of this, but

ALL FOR MOTHER

I have been documenting the difficulties I face every day to my sibling. Everyone believes I have it *so* good. *So* easy. Living rent-free with my mother, the only stipulation being to help her out around the house and with those little things she might need. The *little* things she can't do herself and that my father used to do for her. But those *little* things are not so *little* and not so straightforward. Everything is made more complicated and frustrating by her deteriorating condition. Her words, her mannerisms, and her demands shouldn't grate on me, but they do. It's gotten to the stage where I'm convinced the tsunami of her commands and decrees are drowning me.

I can fight back. Have fought back. Nothing cuts through the pain. It's so tiring to do it again and again and again. Every. Single. Day.

We are each other's captive in this jail of circumstance. No bars to stop us from leaving, only the invisible barrier of our own reasons to stay. Hers is simple. It's her house, and she has nowhere else to go. No aspirations to go out and see the world, to enjoy the sunshine and company of others. She's content, existing in her own little self-built bubble, and although my incursions and battles are played on the outskirts, there's no way this war will be won by me. Even death would be a meaningless victory.

My reasons for being here ... my reasons are countless and are as obscure and illogical as she is. The money is up there as a big motivator. Probably the only one that has me still standing here. The other ones are harder to define, and as time continues to whittle away and any sense of purpose or joy disintegrates, the reasons become less clear, less fluid, and hold less meaning. An early midlife crisis while prisoner to circumstance perhaps. A lonely body seeking their mother's love and reassurance or maybe forgiveness. I'm wondering if I believe she'll wake up one morning and see me. Like, really see me. See my heartache and my needs. For her to reach out with one of her bony arms and clasp her skeletal hand around mine and whisper, *It's all going to be okay*. But she won't, and I suppose this is why I get so angry. Every morning is just like this one.

Just.
Like.
This.
One.

I tell her she's being ridiculous and make a grab for the sheet to pull it back. The grip on the off-white material is absolute as she bemoans how cold and tired she is. She's been awake since one a.m., she says. I nod, feigning compassion, and force my pursed lips to gentle without showing too much teeth. Gritting and biting back my desired responses. Regardless, it's time to get up before the bed is soiled again by an overfilled diaper.

She whines again about how bitterly cold it is and suggests I'm at fault for not providing her an extra blanket. I bite my lip and swallow the retort that desperately wants to slip off the end of my tongue. If I'd told her last night that I raised the temperature, she'd have put up a fuss, saying it wasn't needed. Extra heat uses energy, and energy costs money; because of that, she'd lie between blue-tinged lips and tell me she was warm enough. Forget that she's old and frail and her body doesn't work the way it used to. Circulation is a thing for the youth. But it seems lies and half-truths are things for the elderly.

I pull her up with a bit too much force, and she snaps at me to be gentle and not so rough. Her complaints are overridden by the supposed dizziness that overwhelms her each time she moves from the prone position to sitting. She's nothing but persistent in maintaining her morning soliloquy of earth-spinning proportions.

Trembling arms attempt to push up from the bed. It's a failed effort, and I'm forced again to take her arm and pull her to standing. There's always a moment or two before she gains her equilibrium and we see how bad the day will be. Today won't be that bad as she grips the wheelie walker's handles and shuffles toward the bathroom.

I sigh and wait for her to complete her ablutions.

Every day is the fucking same.

Twenty-Three

The steaming cup of coffee has barely reached my lips when I hear it.

Not again!

The hydraulics of the lift chair lowering and moving position.

There's barely enough time to place the beverage on the counter before she calls out to me. I close my eyes, wishing not for the first time that I could ignore her and take the moment to finish my drink before it chills. But it's no use. I can't call out, asking her to hold on, because she won't acknowledge my words. In the battle of selective hearing, I always lose.

I sigh, push the chair back to stand, and take a moment to watch the heat from my cup slowly dissipate. With a final glance, I bid it good-bye, saying farewell yet again to that longtime lover. It'll be cold and bitter when I return.

Such a waste.

TWENTY-FOUR

She calls out tentatively. When I answer, she is visibly startled, saying she thought I'd already gone to the store. I smile, grinding my molars hard to stop myself from saying something sarcastic and potentially vile to her. She quickly looks away and goes back to watching the ridiculous game show on the television. I stand beside her chair for a moment more, watching the subtitle scroll across the screen before backing quietly into the shadows of the room.

I don't want to go to the store. I don't want to pick up the items she wrote on the list. If she would only go to bed, I could get on with my plans for the evening—texting Joel—but she has it in her head that she needs some peanut brittle.

The Valium I'd placed on the side table with the glass of water has been left untouched. It's a game of wills at this point, her to stay up and punish me by eating the sickly saccharine candy. The sticky sweet adheres to her dentures and requires an extra ten or so minutes of scrubbing. It's a punishment—or a challenge—with the brittle, a pawn to demonstrate who's in control, to show the power of authority, a semblance of being in charge.

But … I'm in charge, not her. The sooner she realizes that, the better.

Twenty-Five

I'm not sure, but I think incontinence is catching. I never thought it could be passed on through contact or by air particles, but it must. Perhaps my urethra has synced to those around me and is now in line with the moon's phasing, much like they claim menstruation does. Either that or my bladder has developed some sort of Stockholm syndrome and is urinating in tandem with my captor.

That would totally be my luck.

Twenty-Six

"Ash."

I can't do this anymore.

My life is one long, ridiculous ride on a Ferris wheel. The music blares on an endless loop of loud carnival music. I'm waiting for it to stop, so I can jump off. My only hope is that when the ride finally does come to a standstill, my carriage will be swinging at the top.

Twenty-Seven

The stone mortar and pestle are already on the kitchen counter when I start preparing her evening meal. I don't blink an eye about the fact that I'm here. Again. I live in a perpetual state of food preparation, waste disposal, and pill-popping. If I'm not in the bathroom, I am here.

It wasn't long ago she'd have a conniption if anyone dared eat or drink in a room not designated for eating. But I don't care. Her laziness and my willingness to bolster it over the past weeks work to my advantage. While she sits in her recliner chair in the shuttered sunroom, monitoring the evening game shows and waiting to be served, I make my arrangements.

My plan is to have her fed, changed, and in bed in under two hours. It's a tight turnaround but totally doable if she's copasetic. My plan hinges on her being agreeable. Not that she really has a choice these days.

He's been ignoring my messages.

I know it's because he's frustrated that I can't get away to see him as often as we'd like. It's not like I have a choice. My mother's care is all-consuming, scorching me from the inside, threatening to leave only charcoaled remains. If it wasn't for him, I'd be nothing but an empty humanoid husk, operating on auto and barely able to function. He's the only thing that has gotten me through these dark days. Him and the occasional pain medication.

But I've come up with a plan to catch up tonight. He was hesitant initially, but I told him it was fine. I need to see him, and as always, I want a break from her. His recent game of playing hard to catch is cute but no longer required, and the sooner he realizes it, the better.

I'm ready to be his.

I'm ready to move on, and I want it to be with him. Our lives together will be perfect.

But first ... *her.*

He fully understands the world I'm submerged in with caring for her, and I'm so thankful for that. Our paths might have crossed at one of the lowest points in my life, but he's picked me up and given me a reason for ... being.

I love my mother.

I hate my mother.

I love to hate my mother. Maybe I love but do not like my mother.

But I can't deny that my tumultuous relationship with her has brought me to this wonderful man that I'm eager to call mine. He knows all my shortcomings, and he knows hers. I think, because of this, he's slightly more cautious about our rendezvous.

It's sweet.

He cares.

For me.

And for her. But I can't have her coming between us anymore. She's meddling even if she's totally in the dark and she doesn't realize it.

It's too much, and it has to stop, but first, I have to get her down for the night.

Down and out for the count. That would be the best outcome. And I know just the right concoction that'll work.

ALL FOR MOTHER

The room is crowded, and I push my way over to the bar and order a drink. It's not the usual atmosphere I enjoy. Too much testosterone huddled around the large screens showing various competing sports teams.

But it's where he said he'd be.

Or the receptionist at the clinic.

It doesn't matter who told me; it only matters that I'm here now.

I see him before he sees me, chatting with a pretty blonde. He's beautiful, and I can tell she thinks so too. My mind is desperate to go down the paranoia path, wondering if this could be the reason he's not been taking my calls.

It's Mother's fault. Her fault I haven't been able to do the things I really want to do. Her fault I've become more and more reliant on chemical supplements to get me through the days. They might help numb the mind, but on occasion, they turn me into a drone.

Maybe that's why Joel's been ignoring my calls. I'm nothing more than a drone for a crone. Uninteresting. Pathetic. Boring. Useless.

"Hey." I tap him on the shoulder, interrupting their conversation.

"Ash. You made it," he says, reaching out to wrap an arm around me and hugging me in close to his side.

The warmth of his lips on my temple immediately chases away the negative thoughts.

"This is …"

The pregnant pause as Joel attempts to remember the blonde's name is embarrassingly laughable. For her.

Her eyes flinty, she puckers her lips up in annoyance as she fills in the blank. "Emily."

"Of course." He shakes his head with a chuckle. "Ash, meet Emily. She works in real estate and was explaining the local market to me. She's quite knowledgeable."

I bet.

"How lovely."

She studies the body language between Joel and myself, and I see the moment when she realizes we're together.

"Oh, wow. I didn't notice it was so late. I have to go. Lovely meeting you, Joel. Here are my details if you're ever in the market." She hands him the small, rectangular card and hitches her handbag higher onto her shoulder before turning. "Nice to meet you, Ash."

Her abrupt exit makes me giggle, and Joel takes my hand in his before looking around the bar. Cheers and catcalling erupt in one corner as a goal is scored, the energy and noise seemingly doubling.

"This place is too loud. Let's get out of here." He nudges me in the side. "I want to hear all the stories I've missed during my week from hell. Sorry about that, for not calling you back."

I don't mind one bit, and I willingly follow him out of the bar.

We belong together.

If only we could be together.

Twenty-Eight

I send another quick text message to Joel, letting him know how much fun I had last night and how I hope we can meet up again soon. Tonight maybe. Spending time outside of this house allowed me to take a breath. Pity it only lasted for those few short hours. In the wilting oppressiveness of the desert that represents my current life, he is my oasis. He bathes me in hope for something better with just his presence alone. I need that more than anything right now with this day in, day out drudgery.

The sharp trill of the home phone startles me, and I lunge for it before it has the chance to ring again. Mother's taking her mid-morning nap, and no one wants to wake a sleeping dragon. Ever.

"Hello?"

"Hello. It's Terry Hurst from Preston and Crossley Law Firm. I'm returning Mrs. Doyle's call. Is she available?"

I quietly tiptoe toward the sunroom to peer inside, but the soft rumble of her snores apprises me of her current state without me having to physically enter and check. Softly, I close the door and walk back to the kitchen.

"I'm sorry. She's indisposed at the moment. Can I help you?"

A chill runs through my body when the caller doesn't respond straightaway. The fractional pause catches my interest as my intuition sends a flare, telling me to take action.

"You're speaking with Ash. Ash Doyle." No immediate response. "Elizabeth is my mother. I'm staying here, helping out after her fall."

"Hey, Ash. I didn't realize she had one of you living with her at the moment."

One of you?

His turn of phrase, talking about Bel and myself, is strange, and he sounds unusually surprised that I'm here. As though I'm not meant to be. I know I wish I were anywhere, but …

"That's right. I've been here since the funeral," I answer.

Why is the lawyer calling here? And returning her call—when did she contact him? My thoughts collide as one, trying to gain understanding and the importance of this conversation.

"Shouldn't you be speaking with Bel? She's been dealing with all of Father's estate and insurance matters."

There's another hesitation, and I can't explain the tingling sensation pushing the hair on the back of my neck up. This Terry has not really said anything, but every bone in my body is behaving like this is a bad omen.

"So, can I help you with anything? I normally send all the bills and paperwork that come in the mail to Bel. Is this about the insurance in probate? I thought Bel was dealing directly with you guys."

"No, it's okay. I can call back later."

This is weird.

"Is everything fine? It sounds like there's something going on. Are you sure I can't help?"

"You know, Ash," he drawls out my name the way you'd call out a petulant child, "I can't discuss this with you. I really need to speak to your mother."

I scratch the itch forming on the back of my neck, and my teeth sink down into my bottom lip. Something's definitely going on, and I don't understand what.

"Oh, okay," I say, cautiously keeping my tone neutral and choosing my words carefully. "I can get Mom to call you back when she's awake. Will that work? Does she have your number?"

Obviously, she does.

What is Mother up to? What game is she playing?

"That would be great. Thank you. And, yes, she does."

He hangs up, and the high I was on from my night with Joel evaporates.

Joel.

I type another note to him and cringe at the words on the screen after they're sent.

Something's up with Mother.

The blue bubbles of text line the screen like obedient soldiers, and I don't bother adding in another to put my last words into context.

Why hasn't he responded to any of my messages?

As I chew on my thumbnail, worrying it down to the quick and biting into the adjacent fleshy skin, the dull throb settles me. My mind is scattered, and I'm finding it hard to follow any definite thread. I find the half-empty bottle of Jack at the back of the pantry and take a swig before sending a message to Bel, asking about the lawyer. Her return call is almost instant.

"What's going on?" I say, skipping the normal niceties.

"I'm so sorry, Ash," Bel says over the phone. "The money's cleared probate, but I can't give you the amount we agreed on."

If the money's cleared, it should be the easiest thing in the world to arrange. Money transfer, check, or cash. It would be as simple as a phone call to organize. Unless this is something else …

Is this why the lawyer was calling?

"How much then?"

The silence hangs heavily, and I know what she's going to say before she breaks it. It was all too good to be true when she promised me the world. Too good. Not true.

"Nothing. I'm so sorr—"

I hang up. There's nothing more to be said. Deep down, I always knew.

Mother.

A quick check confirms she's still sleeping off her breakfast. *Lazy bitch.*

I enter the formal dining room at the front of the house and flick through the stack of mail, wondering what I've missed. What Bel's missed. Most of it is promotional material, like brochures from stores, showcasing sales and seasonal collections. I've hardly looked at any of it in detail in weeks. The letters delivered yesterday are still bound in elastic, and with new eyes, I slowly pull them free to sort through them.

A nondescript white envelope with a simple typed address didn't give me pause when I retrieved it from the mailbox, but now, I study it in more detail. Before overthinking it, I slide my finger down the seam and pull out the papers inside. Hands shake as I read words from the lawyer—the one who just called—confirming my mother wants to gift all of Father's insurance money to the church once it's out of probate.

What the ...

Why?

None of this makes sense. *Have I been walking blind?*

I crumble into one of the chairs and lay my head in my hands on the table. Eyes closed, I try to piece together the fragments from the past weeks that might have indicated that Mother and Bel were up to something.

Bel.

Did she not know, or did she just string me along to care for Mother because no one else was able or wanted to?

She couldn't have known; she wouldn't do this to me.

Or would she?

ALL FOR MOTHER

The pain from banging my head against the table feels so good in contrast to the confusion and numbness dwelling inside of me.

"Ash!"

Why can't she stay asleep or be silent for an hour and let me process everything?

You'd think the lawyer's call and my sister's latest update would've been the signal for her to just shut up this once. I haven't told her I'm now aware of everything, but I know she knows. She's probably been behind this ruse all of this time.

"Ash?"

My feet drag across the carpet as I come to a stop in front of her. She looks at me and purses those thin little lips. Lips that were blue a few months ago as she teetered on the cusp of death. I don't feel guilty about wishing, not for the first time, that I was never in the house that day she fell.

"Yes, Mother."

She must see the fight has gone from me. The cold deadness inside has paralyzed me. I see now that her patience is what's going to win this war for her. Since I've been caring for her, I've often thought about this role reversal of the child becoming the parent. Like any toddler, she has her good days and bad days, as do I. But she's weathered the Ash who's lashed out by being mean. Now, there's nothing left, and she's had her ultimate revenge. She has what she wants.

"My boot's rubbing again on the heel. Can you change the sock and add some padding? It hurts."

The Velcro comes apart with ease from the constant use, and I carefully pull the boot off. Zombie-like, I find another sock to replace the old. There's nothing wrong with the sock, but I put it on, as asked.

I don't know what to say about any of this. I'm at a crossroads. I'm mad, and I'm angry. I'm also sad. I feel trapped by everyone's betrayal and wish I could erase the person that I am and dissolve into nothingness.

If only I could become a shell of a human, then everyone could get what they needed from me, and I would feel nothing. Bel. Mother ... Joel.

I'd feel nothing.

Nothing.

The sum total to what or who I am ...

Is nothing.

I'm not sure if I can survive this for much longer. It's not one thing; a single thing is bearable. It's the multitude of everything weighing down on me, suffocating me.

I'm being eaten alive.

One bite ...

One jab ...

One sting doesn't have the power to kill me, but all of them together will peck me to death.

Destroy me.

And leave me with ... as ... nothing.

I am nothing.

I replace the boot and leave the room.

I can't do this anymore!

It's the latest of the unanswered bubbles on my phone. I sent it, again without thinking, wanting—no, *needing* some sort of connection with someone who could understand. Someone who would take my side. Tell me everything would be okay.

The hydraulics of Mother's chair activates, and I move farther down the hall to the opposite side of the house, not wanting to see her. Her world has become limited to mainly the sunroom and her bedroom and bathroom, leaving me with the rest of the house to hide.

ALL FOR MOTHER

My phone continues to hold my attention, and I stare at the vacant space where his response should be, silently begging him to answer. Three small dots appear, and I let out a huge breath.

He's there.

I wait for his words to materialize, but they don't.

One minute.

Two minutes.

Three minutes.

My mouth dries, and my chest tightens. *How could he do this to me?*

Four minutes.

I wipe an errant tear and take two steps when the phone rings, and my finger silences it a heartbeat later.

"Hey," I mumble into the receiver.

"Hey yourself. I have nine missed calls, three voice mails, and twenty-two text messages from you this morning. Is there something wrong with your mom? Is everything okay?"

"No," I answer simply. My life's falling apart, and Joel's first concern is about Mother. "Nothing's okay."

The silence is broken on my end with the telltale clicking of Mother's wheeled walker. The boot dragging and audible breathing alert me that she's headed my way. I open the hall closet, not wanting her to find me, and close the door behind me, leaning against the back wall.

"Ash?" His honeyed voice is the warmth I'm so desperate for.

"Ash?" Her questioning tone from behind the timber barrier burns my ears, and I slide down to the floor and wrap my arms around my knees.

"Ash?" he asks.

"Ash?" she says louder, the boot scraping along the floor, getting closer.

"Yes," I answer softly to the only one that matters.

"Ash, where are you?" Joel lowers his voice to match mine, concern lacing his words.

"I'm nowhere. Nowhere important."

"What's going on?"

"Nothing. I-I don't think I can do this anymore."

He lets out a breath and clicks his tongue. I don't understand the frustration I'm sensing from him. "Do what?"

"Mother," I say in a hushed whisper as I sense her stopping outside the door. "I hate being here. I hate … her."

"No, nonsense. This is all normal. You're doing fi—"

The bright light from the door opening cuts off the rest of his words as I drop the phone into my lap and shield my eyes.

"Why in the blazing glory are you sitting in the closet?" Mother tsk-tsks. Her delicate frame towers over me as she looks down with an ugly twist to her mouth. "I'm hungry. Is it time for lunch?"

Of course. There's never any privacy, and it's always about her. I bite back the snarl of my smart response, not wanting to start an argument while I know Joel is listening.

"Yes, Mother." I push up from the floor and step around her, bringing the phone back up to my ear. "Joel, I have to go. Can I see you tonight? I love you."

I hang up before he can respond as Mother starts talking from behind me.

"Who is that? Joel? Joel from the doctor's office? Was he calling about my next appointment? Why are you being so secretive, talking to him?"

I turn to look at her and see her trying to piece together a scenario from my stolen conversation. I see when it all clicks in place.

Her lips curl up in disgust. "Unless … no, no, no. You stay away from him, Ash. Do you hear me? He's not for you. He's too good for you, and you'll just end up ruining his life."

My eyes drop to the floor, tears blurring my vision. Her words echo those said years ago, and my heart slowly fills with a burning fire. When I look back up, I swear an apparition of my father is standing at her shoulder. His loathing look and her disapproval are more than I can handle. My jaw clenches so fucking tight that the pain is felt all the way to my ears and down to my toes. I turn away from her and walk to my room.

Fuck Father.
Fuck her.
Fuck them all.

Twenty-Nine

It's time.

The supplies are gathered and lined up on the bed.

Small plastic baggies with its powdered contents, the result of my long-term pill-shaving regime, sit alongside the cold metal relic. They appear alluring and sinister against the backdrop of the patterned duvet. Evil wrapped in the guise of goodness due to its ability to provide salvation. Or is it good wrapped in an evil disguise?

It's happening tonight.

Anticipation creeps in from all angles, and for the first time in a long time, I feel jubilant. The orchestra that'll be set in motion tonight will finally set me free. It might be seen to some as drastic measures, but I know there are those who will understand, who will support this course of action. It's a win-win. She gets to move on with a life after death and reunite with her husband—my excuse for a father. And I get … I get to end this madness.

I get my freedom.

And if the tempo is exactly right, no one will be the wiser. My fingers caress the stock of my father's pistol, knowing its music will play for me—and for her. It's not central to tonight's show but a trusty understudy to be called out just in case.

A flash in the mirror above the chest of drawers shows the reflection of someone almost unrecognizable. A person who's been missing since the innocence of youth was ripped away when the real world decided to reveal its ugly true colors. Wide, clear eyes replace the dull and lifeless of those that normally stare back. A pinch of color is added to the cheeks along with a ... smile—something that's been absent for quite a while.

I admire my treasure trove once more, mentally going through the plan, congratulating myself for my brilliance thus far. Even the air inhaled is tainted with excitement. The wrist-worn clock face shows the time is nigh. Minutes force the hour hand to make the jump forward, whether it wants to or not. For me, time is a friend, and the gentle persuasion of the watch's second hand is nothing but sweet inducement for what is to come.

A high-pitched sound summons me. I take one more moment to study the face in the mirror before schooling my expression and grabbing my instruments of deliverance.

My feet barely kiss the threshold before her demands begin.

"Tea. Get me some hot tea, will you? And don't forget to put it on a saucer, with a napkin," she says without raising her eyes from the book held in her lap. "I'm cold, and my bones are aching. Can you check the thermostat as well?"

Yes, mein Führer. *At once.*

An orange tinge lines the outside of the window, fighting to obtain access through the crevices of the closed shutters. Those rays that get through cast eerie shadows across the room, moving as the trees outside sway with the breeze. The setting couldn't be more perfect.

"Of course, Mother."

With a sweep of my hands and a flourished bow, I become the maestro and begin.

There is no turning back.

ALL FOR MOTHER

After delivering the tea and turning the temperature up to ninety, I peruse the contents of the kitchen, wondering, if given a choice, what she'd choose as her last meal. If she knew death was imminent, what would she pick? If I had to choose for myself, I'd forgo all the formality of fine dining and go with a tray of gooey double-stuffed Oreo and cookie dough chocolate brownies. Straight from the oven. Nothing like a sugar high to give the boost necessary to stare death directly in its eyes during those final moments.

For her tonight, I've chosen something simple that I know she'll eat without question and something I can easily lace with the drugs. Make her compliant, unable to resist what is to follow. She's a sucker for macaroni and cheese, and the colorless, cheesy goo will mix well. The issue will be the taste.

So far, I've gotten away with adding a few things here or there, but tonight's cocktail will be unlike anything she's had before. I taste-test just to be sure.

It's going to be wonderful. A magical ending no one predicted to a tragic tale. And I'll have the best seat in the house.

When she closes her eyes for the last time, tongue unable to form any words, I will be the last image she sees. She will know it was me. That I was responsible. And she will know why.

She's lucky I'm giving her the option of the harmless way out. She will feel no pain. She'll just float away and be no more …

No one will wonder why or how. There'll be no autopsy. No questions.

Just another old widow whose time came.

And then I can begin again and become someone.

"Here you go. Dinner."

The cold hardness against my back when I sit reminds me not to fidget. I'm here with one purpose only. To watch the demise of my mother. To have her listen to my truth and to say good-bye. To close this chapter and open the next.

"I'm not in the mood for pasta. Can you get me some soup and then maybe some ice cream?"

Of course she'd try to thwart me. It's in her nature to take control. But not tonight.

"Eat the mac 'n' cheese, and I'll get you some ice cream." I should be given an award for keeping my calm. For not pulling out the gun and demanding her to eat. But I don't want to play my hand too early. I need her to eat. "There's no soup."

"Okay." She spoons a mouthful, and with her mouth, she continues to talk, "You should go to the store and get some more soup later."

I nod and humor her by pretending to listen. She spoons another mouthful and then tells a story.

Spoon. Story. Spoon. Story.

Until it's gone.

She pushes the plate away and looks at me expectantly. I remain a statue and watch her, waiting for something to happen.

"Can I have my ice cream now?"

"No."

"No?" she asks, exasperated. "Why not?"

After all this time, she still talks to me like this. Treats me like this. It's a pity she's my mother and that it's taken me all of this time to work out what needs to be done. The money might have clouded my judgment, but it's not there anymore.

There's no money. No life. The only certainty is Mother. And death.

Thirty

"Why are you being like this?"

"Like what?" I say as I pause my pacing, perplexed. I didn't realize I'd started wearing a path in the carpet. I turn to look at her, stranded in her seat. Helpless. "Like me? This is me. This is who I am."

I'm vexed the drugs haven't kicked in the way they were meant to. Tension's rippling through my body, and I tug on my earlobe in frustration. The immediate, sharp pain doesn't bring the clarity I was aiming for.

"No, this isn't you, Ash. You're being ugly right now." Her words hang in the air, and I expect it won't be long before the crocodile tears come. Already, her face is blotchy. "Ugly to me."

"Just stop talking." I pull the gun from the back of my pants and brandish it in her direction. "Talking, talking, talking. You never know when to shut up."

"Ash—"

"Just shut up! I need to think."

The room seems so distant, blurred around the edges. Crouching, I bring my hands to my head. The cool of the hard metal feels so good against my temple. It reminds me why I'm here. Why we're here. I focus in on her. Her breathing's shallow and coming in quick now.

Finally.

"You know, it didn't need to be this way. I never wanted it to get to this stage. But I really think this will be good for you. Surely, you don't want to continue on like this?" Standing, I wave my arms in her direction. At her, sitting in her chair. Always sitting in her fucking chair. "I'm ending your suffering. I'm doing you a favor, don't you see? It's more than anyone in this family has done for me."

"That's a lie. We've always been here for you. We've always ... tried." Her last word is strained, almost a question. She knows it's not entirely the truth.

"Sure, Mom. Sure you did," I say with a forced laugh. "It doesn't matter now. You'll be in a better place soon."

"Where's all this hatred coming from, Ash? Where?" she says with exasperation. "What have I ever done to warrant this hate?"

I sigh. The inventory of the family's transgressions is far too long to list. There's simply not enough time. And it's not as though I hate them. Or her. Disappointment and sadness are the emotions I'd pin toward family. But in this moment, it's not about them. It's about her.

And as much as I wish I could, I don't hate her. Far from it. She's my mother. But the circumstances ... it's the circumstances I can't deal with anymore. Moving in here, living under the same roof as her, was probably the worst decision I've ever made—and I've made a lifetime of bad fucking decisions. I probably should've stayed where I was, worked it out with my job, or applied for a new position. I could've lived out of my car or done another round of couch-surfing. It might've worked. I might've ended up back on my feet.

Why did I come home? Why did I feel the need to revisit all these emotions that I'd been desperately trying to run away from for over two decades? It's not as though any of them have ever taken the time to understand me. I've always felt like the black sheep, the dirty little secret hidden behind the stupid plantation shutters.

ALL FOR MOTHER

"I honestly thought things would be different after Dad's death. I don't know why or what I was expecting. I thought you felt the same way—that we could somehow make amends for the past and find the closeness we hadn't had when I was growing up."

I turn my back on her and open the shutters to look out at the night sky. Clouds are moving in, slowly blanketing the stars. I smirk at her intake of breath and anticipate her next words to tell me to shut them. I glance over my shoulder, daring her to speak. The look on my face has her swallowing whatever words she was about to say. I laugh silently and turn to watch as the final few stars disappear. Suddenly switched off, as though they'd blinked out of existence. Just like she will be tonight.

The harsh crack of the shutters closing makes her flinch. Her eyes meet mine for a second before traveling down toward the gun in my hand. She visibly swallows and sits back in the chair, struggling to maintain a sense of calm. But we both know she's anything but. Her feeble mind is struggling to think. To assess. She's attempting desperately to come up with a plan. To work out what to say. To try and talk her way out of the predicament she's gotten herself into.

"I honestly thought I was doing the right thing, coming here to help you," I say softly. Calmly. "But instead, you've only succeeded in keeping me away from life. *My* life. It's as though you're trying to pull me toward death with you."

I shake my head, endeavoring to extinguish those thoughts. I'm not ready to die. *I've* got everything to live for. Not like her. She's standing at death's door, and she can't escape that reality. A few months ago, nothing about this situation, this *job*, would've bothered me. I would have gladly moved forward with her. But not now. Now, I have this opportunity. A chance for *my* happily ever after.

Her words are spoken softly. Hesitantly. Her nervousness showing with the care taken to enunciate each word. "But ... I thought you wanted to help m—"

I don't let her finish. I don't need her to guilt me out of following through with my plan. Her manipulations won't work here tonight.

"I'm not a nurse, Mom," I say, frustrated. "Never in my life have I ever wanted to be a nurse. Nor am I a geriatric caregiver."

Spittle sprays, and I wipe my mouth with the back of my arm, not dropping eye contact with her. A tingling sensation creeps along my back with the increasing dampness of my shirt. I clench my jaw and halt the pacing I didn't realize I'd started again. The air in the room is stifling, and I berate myself for turning the heat up so high. It's meant to affect her, not me.

"By God, I've tried. I've tried. I wanted it to work. But little by little, you've stripped my identity away. Forced me to do your bidding, to be your slave." My voice hitches, and I hurriedly swipe away the moisture gathered on my face. "I never signed up for this. I *never* signed up for this at all. I never wanted to see you naked, to change your diapers, to wash your soiled garments and sheets. That was not part of the deal. It was just meant to be free lodging in exchange for occasional companionship. Not a twenty-four/seven goddamn maid service."

The indignant look on her face makes me want to laugh, and I run my hand through my hair, taking a deep breath. Out of everything that's gone down tonight, it's talk about her adult diapers that ruffles her feathers. The fact that I have a gun and she's stranded in a chair with no escape unsettles her and upsets her. But my mention of seeing her naked and dealing with her excrement is what catches her ire.

I walk to stand directly in front of her, my tall frame casting a shadow across her face. She won't look at me, her gaze remaining studiously beyond my right hip. Rapid eye flutters now match the short, sharp, rapid breaths.

I want her to look at me.

I will her to look at me.

"My life was already in tatters, but at least I had some hope that it could be better," I say softly. Unexpected, the gentleness of these words has her raising her head toward mine. "You've stolen that away from me. You've shown me death. You've shown me mortality."

She shakes her head in denial.

"You took advantage of me," I continue. "I want to be angry. I want so hard to be angry with you, to hate you, but for whatever reason, I can't. I pity you. Pity who you are and what you've become. What you always have been."

"I've shown you love." Her voice cracks, and a bony hand moves to swipe away the wetness glistening under her eyes. It's an effort, and watching the slow, jerky movements makes me want to slap it down. She's pathetic.

"You've never shown me love," I scoff, offended by her weak words. "What love have you shown me? What? When? I had to grow up, watching all the affection ... all the care, and the love you showed my sister, her friends, our cousins. But not me. Never me."

"That's not true." It's her turn to take offense. "You were always following your father around. You idolized him. You belonged to him."

Her words freeze me. My grip on the handgun tightens, squeezing ...

"I. Did. Not. Belong. To. Him," I say, articulating every word with a hatred that's been fermenting for years. Feelings bubbling below the surface, scarring from the inside.

"This is not about him," I say slowly, my voice deep, dark. "This is about you. You're no better than him. I thought you'd be different, that due to the circumstances, you'd see me. The real me. But you haven't. You've taken me for granted and used and abused me, just like everyone else."

I pause for a second, letting the harshly spoken words settle in the room.

They're not completely true. *He* doesn't treat me like that. *He* appreciates me. It's because of Joel and the love we have for each other—organic, undiluted, and pure— that I've reached this point. I've seen and felt what it's like to be needed and cared for, and it's been all too brief.

I want more.

But I can't have it if she's still here, dictating the circumstances of my life. Nagging me. Cajoling me. Playing with sensibilities and emotionally draining me. Treating me like a dog instead of one of the children that she brought into this world.

"Every day, I thank you for your hard work, and I tell you that I love you—"

"What?" I interrupt. I don't want to hear her reasoning, her excuses. I don't need to hear any more of those. "Those little confessions as you lie in bed, wondering if it's your last night on earth. Trying to confess your sins and leave this world with a clean slate. That's not love. That's you pretending you're some pious, old lady. I hate those. Hate them. They're insincere and more about you than me, more about you trying to manipulate and justify your stupid actions for the day and ask for forgiveness. Well, how about this? I don't forgive you."

I stop still in front of her and scream, "I. Don't. Forgive. You!"

Her pallor changes to a sickly white. It's yet to get to that translucence I know from the last time she kissed death but didn't embrace it. I kept the Reaper at bay that time, but I'll not make the same mistake today.

I stand in silence and watch. Labored breaths hitch on the end, eyes fearful, furtively darting around. Ever so slowly, a hand rises to clutch her chest.

Finally.

ALL FOR MOTHER

This point is the culmination of what was put in play this morning, preparing her body to move on into the afterlife. To get her just deserts. Meet her maker. Only death can set her free, and death is here now, untying the anchors shackling her to this world.

And I couldn't be more jubilant.

THIRTY-ONE

The fear on her face makes me smile. I close my eyes to help still my mind in preparation for the next stage of her soul's spiritual journey, wondering if I'll feel it's departure. She doesn't deserve the strength and comfort that comes with the church's interpretation of last rites, and I feel a smug satisfaction that she won't get to have her sins forgiven. I might've listed her sins, but I certainly won't forgive them.

"Take her, God. Take her," I mutter over and over again, turning my ramblings into a reverent prayer. I pray for a quick death, mainly for it to be over so I can get back to my life. I pray to Saint Joseph, the patron of departing souls, asking him to allow her to suffer just a little bit, telling him that she deserves the misery.

"What the fuck, Ash!"

Breath whooshes from my body as my shoulder is jostled, and I'm knocked out of the trance. Confusion must be written over my face as my eyes open to see a broad back clad in medical scrubs, bent over my mother's chair. Strong hands hold her frail ones, and his head bends toward her face.

A gasp escapes as he turns, and I see the worry etched on his face. "Call 911. She's going into cardiac arrest."

Joel.

My feet are glued to the floor as I watch his ministrations. The confidence and sureness of his movements as he deals with my mother, trying to save her.

Save. Her.

No.

"Ash! C'mon! She can't breathe," Joel says, taking a moment to break eye contact to watch my mother suffocate. His forced breaths almost match her deafening attempts to suck air into her lungs.

One of his hands disappears into a pocket to pull out a phone. The screen lights, and his fingers are poised, ready for action. I can't let him call the authorities. Not yet. Not until it's time. Not until I know she's dead.

"Joel, move away from my mother." Venom laces my words. I take a step back and aim the gun in his direction.

"What the fuck? Let me call an ambulance," he says, voice shaking.

He looks upset, but that's probably because he doesn't quite understand. How could he? He was never privy to my intentions for tonight—for her. This is a recent development. I kept it that way for a reason.

For a surprise. For us.

"Joel. Slowly ... move away from her," I repeat, voice deadly quiet. My body's alive, buzzing with electricity under the skin's surface. Eyes narrow, twitching slightly, when he doesn't immediately respond. "Drop the phone. I mean it. I don't want to, but I will shoot."

His hand stills, and he slowly pivots in his crouch to look up at me. Surprise flashes through his eyes before puzzlement settles in. Unbelieving.

"What's going on, Ash?" he questions quietly, allowing the phone to fall onto the floor at his feet and raising his hands slowly in front of him.

He unhurriedly rises to stand, careful not to lose eye contact. My mother's body twitches intermittently, her eyes wide in horror. Barely audible gasps of pain coming from her are masked by the increasing sound of blood pumping through my body.

"Ash, let me help her. She can't breathe." His voice is low and ragged.

"I know." A chuckle escapes, following my words. I can't help it.

I'm teetering on being ecstatic, knowing it'll all be over soon, yet I'm also baffled by his presence. Unsettled. Him being here was not part of the plan. But the plan is about us. About our future. Him being here can't be all that bad.

"Isn't it wonderful? Everything will be over soon. Everything will work out. This is it—the moment we've been waiting for. Once she's gone, there's nothing holding us back."

He's what will make all of this worthwhile ...

The look of confusion morphs into anger. His muscles tighten across his scrubs as his shoulders pull back, and he stands up straighter. He's magnificent.

"Let me call a damn ambulance," he says, eyes narrowing and softening slightly as they meet mine. Pleading.

Pleading for *her*.

For *her* life.

"No." I shake my head and put my growing frustration aside. "No. She has a medical directive that says not to resuscitate. She just has to ride it out…"

"I don't think she has a directive allowing her to be murdered. Are you crazy?" he growls, clenching his fists, knuckles whitening.

His words halt me. The smile previously plastered across my face is wiped clear. I watch, motionless, as his eyes momentarily glance down toward the discarded phone on the floor before rising back to hold mine. There's a hard glint present, and I don't like it. Don't like it at all. The serene feeling I was holding on to minutes before his arrival is gone. The contentment I felt as she closed in on those gates of hell—or God forbid, heaven—

is gone. A future with him is now potentially gone too. She has stolen everything.

Gone.

"Step away from her. Step the fuck away," I snarl, the words low and harsh.

He hasn't broken eye contact with me, and I don't want to look down. I don't want to confirm the fear that he's betrayed me. That he managed to make a call before dropping the phone. Instead, I continue looking at him. His mien is one I'm familiar with. It's the one I see in the mirror when I think of my mother and how she's been strangling life out of me. I don't like this look on his face. It's all wrong. It's not him.

It's not my Joel.

My lips pinch while my back teeth grind together. At this moment, I don't think I can trust him. My gut's telling me that I've missed something monumental, and I'm not sure what it is.

I can't trust him.

I want so very much to trust him.

"What did you do?" I ask softly, desperately hoping I'm wrong.

He blinks at my question, eyes creasing in disappointment before hardening again. His jaw juts out in challenge. He's not asking for forgiveness, but giving me all the acknowledgment I need of his betrayal.

But I need him. I'm doing this for him. For me. For us.

I let out a deep breath. This will work itself out. It has to. He needs to see that I'm right. I'm right to be doing this. He has to come around. With time, he will.

"Ash," he says gently, jaw relaxing slightly as he takes a deep breath of his own.

Finally ... he sees it.

"Everything will work out. It's all going to be okay," I say lightly, gun wavering. "Once she's gone, we'll be free. Her death will set us free."

ALL FOR MOTHER

This is Joel, I remind myself. He'll understand. He'll understand the sacrifices I've made to get to this point. He'll be thankful once he realizes what's going on. I just need to explain it to him.

Again.

He just needs to think it through. To hear my words. He'll get it.

"What did you give her?" he asks calmly.

I laugh, lowering the gun. "What she deserved."

"No, I mean it. I want to know. What did you give her?"

He shoots a quick glance toward my mother. I follow his gaze and note her eyes are glazed, staring off at nothing.

It won't be long now.

"Valium. Codeine. Digoxin. Nitroglycerin. Ecstasy. Penicillin."

I'm in a trance, watching her veins change color against her papery skin. My words, listing the various drugs I was able to scrape together, sound remote and rote. A veritable cocktail of a mishmash of medication.

The room stills, noise siphoned off, leaving us in muted silence.

She doesn't look like she's breathing. There's no movement of her chest. No telltale raising or lowering.

"It's okay, Mrs. Doyle. It's going to be okay," he says softly.

Caringly.

In the same tone he used when consoling me.

But he's using it toward her.

Why is he talking to …

Her finger moves slightly. A slight twitch, followed by the uncurling of fingers.

She's not dead.

Yet.

"Stop it!" I shout, wiping perspiration from my upper lip. It's so hot in here. *Why is it so hot in here?* "Stop talking to her. Why are you here?"

Joel's presence has thrown me off-kilter. The room's staleness from continuously being closed up and occupied by a diaper-wearing old woman has been compromised by his muskiness. The cologne that once brought a smile to my face is now cloying, catching in my throat with the bitter, sweet, saccharine flavor. Added to the heat of the room, my mind spins. Walls appear to move of their own volition.

"You weren't picking up your calls," he whispers after a long moment of silence, attention back on me, words evenly spoken. His lips move up into an attempted smile, which would be endearing if it matched his eyes. They hold a level of wariness that I never wanted to see in them. His eyes flick toward the metal gripped in my hand and down to his feet.

I raise my arm, aiming again toward them. Toward her.

"Ash. What are you doing?" he continues, words strained. He's acting strange.

It could be because of the gun. Maybe he thinks I'd use it against him. I could never do that. I'd never do that.

I lower the weapon, the metal rubbing my jean-clad thigh. I'm so confused.

What's he doing?

This is Joel.

He knows me.

Loves me.

We're going to be together.

Forever.

After *she's* gone.

Why's her death taking so goddamn long?

I raise the gun again.

"You shouldn't be here, Joel. You shouldn't be here," I say with a hint of hysteria.

ALL FOR MOTHER

It should be done. She should be dead. He really shouldn't be here.

"You weren't meant to see this. This was meant to be quick …" My words trail off as I start pacing again. Hands involuntarily run through my hair as I shake my head in disbelief.

His presence is making me lose my mind. My thoughts aren't clear.

He can't be here.

My vision blurs as I start combing through the options available to me. Joel needs to leave. She needs to die. Her death is inevitable. But no one will think twice about it because she's old and it's close to her time. It *is* her time.

"Joel, you need to leave—" I start to say.

Blue and red lights filter through the window and cast an eerie glow on his face. On her face. His expression changes. Again.

I take a hesitant step back, body trembling, and peer through the cracks of the shutters. A small crowd has gathered on the sidewalk outside the boundary of the yard. Two police cars—the reason for the lights—are parked on the road, and officers are gesturing for the nosy neighbors to move on.

"What did you do?" I whisper, not wanting to admit fully to myself that he betrayed me. That he put me at risk like this.

"Ash, you know I love you. But this is wrong," he responds, voice breaking, gesturing toward my mother.

Tears fall freely as a sob escapes my mouth. The grip on the gun loosens, and I lower it in defeat. I can't believe he did this. That he chose her over me.

Her.

Not me.

Never me.

A skeletal arm rises slowly from the chair, and I shake my head in disbelief that through all of this, the bitch is still alive.

Fuck this!

"Why is it that no one ever chooses me?" I say, forcing my shaking arm up, finger tensing on the trigger. Tonight was always going to end one way. I need to ensure it will. "Well, I fucking choose me!"

A look of fear crosses Joel's face, but I ignore him as I place my mother within the sights of the pistol. Time stills, and the noise of his objections falls away. In this moment, there is just me, her, and my father's gun. I close my eyes and fire, happy in the knowledge that whatever happens next, she'll get what she deserves. Air is forced from my lungs as my body's thrown and lands with a hard jolt on the floor, gun flying free from my hold. My head hits hard, and sparks fly beneath my eyes. A guttural groan sounds from the weight holding me down, restricting my ability to take a much-needed breath. Light filters in, and with unfocused eyes, I watch as Joel's fist lowers to connect with my face, forcing me into darkness.

THIRTY-TWO

I struggle and cry out, throat constricting and dry. Ever so dry. It hurts, and my jumbled words exit my airway, as though scored by a knife. My coarse pleas for help go unanswered.

I can't see.

It's so dark.

And it's so, so quiet.

Why is it so dark? Where are the lights?

Will someone please help me and turn on the lights?

Someone?

Anyone?

Mother? Mom?

My mind screams out for my mother, which is hilarious because she can't help me … she's gone. I made sure of that. I curse myself for being nothing other than generic and falling back to the base sense of existence, crying out for my mommy.

I am not that weak.

I am better than that.

Stronger than that. The path I chose to walk made sure of it.

I falter and call for *him* instead.

Joel.

Flashes of color appear, as though beckoned by my call. I take a deep breath, the inhalation cutting as thick as a razor-blade bouquet.

I need to calm down and think.

Calm down.

Think.

My eyes twitch, and slowly, as though I were coming out of a mystical-induced sleep, they struggle to move. Eyelashes glued to my skin peel away lash by lash as I continue with the forced momentum for them to open. I groan at the inconvenience of whatever's going on, tongue lolling uncontrollably around my mouth. Clicking and sucking on the back of my teeth, I subconsciously try to induce enough saliva to coat my mouth and throat. There's a copper taste and something sour ... something off. It's sharp, acidic, and the longer my tongue moves around, the more I taste it. My mouth moistens tenfold, and I choke back on the acrid flavor.

Spluttering, I try to lift my arm to wipe away the spittle, only to find resistance. The pressure around my wrists increase with every sharp tug I make.

I need to open my eyes. I need to see where the hell I am and what the hell is going on.

Holding my breath, I concentrate on my eyelids. Eyebrows lift with the strain of the movement, and a guttural cry is released despite the excruciating pain of my throat.

A kaleidoscope of colors greets me as I rapidly blink away the stickiness and try to take stock of where I am. I can't make out anything other than a few obtuse shapes. They're softened by a glowing light overhead. Garbled sounds come from my right, but it hurts to look. The sting burning my corneas is so bad that I close my eyes.

A sharp prick, and I drift.

ALL FOR MOTHER

It's no longer quiet or dark.

But it smells. Hospital-grade bleach wafts and combines with the *parfum de l'urine*—an aroma I'm more than familiar with.

My eyes peel open, this time without issue, and blink rapidly until I'm able to focus. An abundance of white reflects from the overhead fluorescent tubes, the brightness amplifying the stench. Noting my surroundings, I take a deep breath, and a relieved shudder rolls through my supine body.

I'm in a hospital.

There are restraints holding my arms, restricting any movement. Deep, pulsing pain throbs behind my temples, piercing my ability to think clearly, as I slowly move to see what's constraining me. The coldness circling my wrists are handcuffs chaining me to the side of the bed. I jerk them, groaning from both the exertion and an intensifying headache. Any abating feelings held when I gained consciousness subside, replaced with confusion and fear.

Lying motionless, I concentrate on breathing. In and then out. With each labored breath, my body whispers a story, highlighting various aches, abrasions, and swelling. The dullness of the discomfort sharpens, and the nerve endings of my reposed limbs shoot out and stab until they hit the height of an unseen battle.

Machines beep, inhuman tones increasing the tempo as I move, struggling to alleviate the burning sensations while simultaneously trying to remain as still as possible for the same reason. The conundrum causes me to cry out. There's no clear way to erase the pain.

Shadows pass behind the frame within the door before it opens, and a nurse quickly walks in. Her face studies machines and then the chart. She pens something before she fiddles with the IV to my side that I didn't realize was attached to me.

"What's happened? Where am I? And"—I tug against my metal shackles—"why am I handcuffed to the bed?"

My words are barely above a whisper, my throat hoarse, making them raspy, but I can see from her subtle reaction that she heard and understood me.

"Please ... why?" I try again, fighting the urge to scream from the pain.

"Try to stay still, Mr. Doyle. The morphine will kick in soon." She turns and leaves me alone.

Time slows when the door swings closed, a fraction of a second expanding to what seems like minutes. Hours. A flash of light from movement in the hallway catches my notice, drawing my attention to the shiny weapon amid the dark blue of the uniformed officer. He moved after the nurse exited, not to walk the lit halls, but to stand at duty adjacent to my room.

My vision blurs slightly as the cool liquid from the drip extends to reach through my veins, and I rest my head back with an inhale. The corners of my mouth turn up, and I feel ... happy.

Mother is dead.

She must be for me to warrant an armed guard. Of course I'd have preferred for her to die from drug complications masked by old age. But being a felon doesn't seem as bad as I imagined it would be. Not that I care—as long as she is finally gone. My only regret will be the sacrifice of my budding relationship with Joel while I pay the price for pushing Mother into the grave she was mostly already filling. He might be understanding. No. He will be sympathetic. Once I explain, he'll see that I was right. I'll just have to wait and see ...

What.
Was.
That?

In a fragmented millisecond and just before the door fully shut, I saw it. I swear it was a silhouette of my mother. But it couldn't have been. She's dead. She has to be.

ALL FOR MOTHER

It must be what they're doping me with to control the pain. Morphine, the nurse said. I must be in that sweet spot between hallucination and a dream. Allowing my eyes to close, I settle in for the excursion into oblivion. I can worry about the police and Joel later. When I wake.

Sounds mute and become a low hum of energy. A wave of peace rides up and down, starting at my toes and finishing at the tips of my ears. My jaw slackens, and the muscles around my mouth tingle and somehow pull me inward. It's as if I were levitating in some type of trance above the hospital bed, the serenity something I've never experienced before.

Laughter cuts through my Zen-like state, disrupting the tranquility, forcing me to crash back down to reality. My eyes open and stare at the bland ceiling, my ears working overtime with the tenacity of a wolf amid the wolf pack. A light sheen of liquid forming on the top of my lip and forehead create chills when it meets the overly cool hospital ventilation system.

It can't be her.

Air particles swirl as the door is pushed open, followed by a scuffling step I am more than familiar with. I hold my breath, hoping and praying this is nothing more than a dark nightmare, part of the drug stupor I'm currently in.

"Ashton Robert Doyle."

The words are clear and ring through the silence I so desperately want to keep. I move my head slightly to the left and see ... Mother. There's no opaqueness. I can't see through her. She looks solid, which means it's not some aberrant spirit. This is real.

"Are you feeling okay? You look like you've seen a ghost." She chuckles, leaning into the black aluminum walking stick supporting her frame.

Me too, just in the guise of a little old lady.

"I thought you were dead."

A forlorn look graces her made-up face as she slowly shakes her head. "No, dear. Someone is, but it's not me."

A sharp pang has my eye twitching uncontrollably. I watch through spasming vision as I try to digest her words. I didn't completely think through the actions that had led me to be here. I just thought... assumed that I'd succeeded with ending her life. For her to be standing beside me now while I'm chained to a bed is evidence that something went wrong. Something's not right. If we're both here, then that only means—

It takes a moment, but when my heart splinters, I know the truth without a doubt.

"No!"

I fight through the calm of the morphine, creating torrents of peace in its wake. My body burns numbly as I struggle against the metal shackles, wanting—*needing*—to feel the anguished pain in my bones to mirror that of my soul. My screams bring the nurse into the room, scrambling to inject something into my arm. Mother steps out of the way while the police officer holds me down to allow the nurse to prick me.

My body stills although not through choice. The intruders depart as quickly and quietly as they came, leaving me alone again with Mother and my tortured self. I close my eyes, wanting to shut out the world.

"I tried really hard to forgive you and allowed you a second chance," Mother speaks in a whisper, her words spoken close to my ear. She knows I can hear her but mustn't want others to overhear. "Leviticus says, if a man lies with a male as he lies with a woman, both of them have committed an abomination. They shall be put to death, and their blood is on their own hands."

A tear escapes, slowly tracking down my cheek. I don't want to hear this, but I have no other choice but to listen.

"I wanted you to have changed. But you haven't. You're detestable, an unrepentant sinner."

ALL FOR MOTHER

My eyes slowly open. Through blurry sight, I see her face hovering over mine, lips thin and white, eyebrows scowling.

"Joel's dead. That blood is on you. Death row—that's what you've got to look forward to now," she mutters, no longer really talking to me. "God is never wrong. You were such a good boy. We brought you up to be a good boy. Joel didn't deserve this; you led him astray."

The sedative, mixed with the painkillers, has me wrapped tightly in a warm cocoon. And I'm glad. I don't want to listen to my father's words coming out of her old crone's mouth.

"You're going to get what you deserve. You're going away for a very long time." She moves back with a small, secretive smile and straightens her blouse. Her lecture's almost done. "And when you meet your maker, there'll be a special place in hell waiting for you."

With all the strength I can muster before being pulled under completely, I whisper, "Yes, and I look forward to seeing you there, Mother."

THE END

ACKNOWLEDGMENTS

The idea for this story is hard to pin down. Life is constantly moving and evolving, and with life comes death. My father-in-law passed away late 2018, around the time my family was planning to relocate from Alaska to Australia. It was a very difficult time, as we didn't get a chance to mourn, having to continue full steam ahead with the preparations for the international move. His passing temporarily opened a door for me to explore what has been dubbed as the *sandwich generation*. The short tenure looking into everything that surrounds geriatric care was definitely an eye-opener. I believe Ash's character came about from an extreme emotional connection with the sandwich generation and a sympathy for all involved. I've since lost my father—just as this book was being finalized and with my editor. My father loved the excerpts I'd shared with him during his last visit prior to the pandemic. He got a kick out of the story premise and thought some—not all—of Ash's antics were highly amusing.

My husband has remained my biggest supporter and alpha reader. He patiently listened as I read chapters aloud before we got into a debate over word choices or grammar. As with my last book, he still needs to be reminded that this is a work of fiction and not an academic piece of writing.

K. MOORE

Bre Lockhart, friend and secret keeper. She likes it when I message her at all hours of the day, asking crazy questions or whining about something benign. Bre's the one you want in the car for lengthy road trips across US state borders—because she drives—and as your wingwoman for all things crazy in Vegas. Thank you for your candid replies, my bio, and the discussion questions.

Sandra Dee remains my unicorn, and I still don't know what I bring to our friendship. Since my move, it's like I've had a limb chopped off. I miss our chats, our trips, and our wines.

My beta readers are a motley bunch, who I love dearly. Georgana. Ruth. Amber. Cassie. Leila. Sherrylee. This book would not be here without these wonderful women. They are more than readers; they're my cheerleaders, my confidants, and most importantly, my friends. I can't wait for the borders to reopen, so we can drink moonshine around a fireplace on a mountainside somewhere, talk books and writing, and solve all the mysteries of the world.

Jovana, my editor. And yes, I've added in this line after she's already painstakingly gone through everything. Sorry, not sorry. Thank you for your wisdom and patience.

If you've made it this far, thank you.

I love to read; it's one of my many favorite things. By taking the time to get to this point, we have so much in common.

If you liked this book—or even if you didn't—please leave a review. You might not think it makes a difference, but it does. Reviews—good, bad, or otherwise—tell other people that an author is worth reading. And for indie authors, it's one way to help get our names out there.

Thank you.

Reading Group Guide

1. Based on the title alone, what did you think *All for Mother* would be about?
2. In the opening funeral scene, how would you describe Ash's relationship with the other family members?
3. How would you have described Ash's appearance while reading the first two to three chapters of the book?
4. How did you feel about Ash's love interest, Joel? What about Ash's sister, Bel? What do you think either character added to the story?
5. During the middle, when we see the relationship between Ash and Mother begin to degrade, how did you perceive Mother? Was she a sympathetic character?
6. What three words would you use to describe Ash's mental state by the time the climatic poisoning plan came to fruition?
7. Elder care is an outcome that affects a huge portion of the population, both in the US and abroad. Did this book make you reconsider your own possible future, either as a caregiver or receiver of care?

8. How did the revelation at the end of the story hit you? Did it affect your perception of the characters, their relationships, or their motivations?
9. The end scene showcases a more opinionated and direct version of Mother. What do you think that says about Ash's perception of his mother throughout the story?
10. After the last sentence, how did you feel about the character of Mother? How much did your thoughts on that character change from page one until the end?

ABOUT THE AUTHOR

K. Moore is the author of domestic psychological thrillers, including *All for Mother*, *Desert Rose*, and a novella in a shared world anthology, *Killer at Dark Hollow Lake*.

She currently resides along Australia's Sunshine Coast with her husband, two sons, and their Karelian bear dog named Hathor. In her free time, she enjoys gardening, hiking along the beach, and reading—about the only things one can successfully do during a global pandemic. If you manage to locate a decent bottle of gin and a chair at the bar, she might be convinced to regale you with tales of her global travels. Without the gin, you'll have to find the evidence within the pages of her stories and poetry.

K. MOORE

FIND K. MOORE ONLINE AT:

www.AuthorKMoore.com

www.facebook.com/AuthorKMoore

www.instagram.com/runs2ny

https://twitter.com/runs2ny

Keep up-to-date and sign up for K. Moore's newsletter:

http://bit.ly/kmoorenews

Made in the USA
Monee, IL
25 November 2020